THE GENiUS FiLES

FROM TEXAS WITH LOVE

DAN GUTMAN

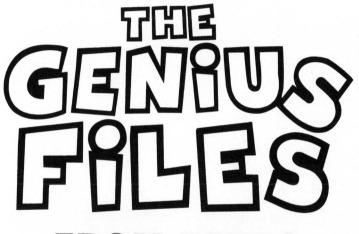

THE GENIUS FILES

FROM TEXAS WITH LOVE

HARPER

An Imprint of HarperCollinsPublishers

ISBN 978-0-06-182773-0 (trade bdg.)
ISBN 978-0-06-182774-7 (lib. bdg.)

Art and typography by Erin Fitzsimmons
13 14 15 16 17   CG/RRDH   10 9 8 7 6 5 4 3 2 1
❖
First Edition

Thanks to Jane Sturdivant Britt, Steve Busti, Trish Carlberg, Christine Feller, Dennis Geoffroy, Emma Gutman, Andrew Harwell, Sarah Kaufman, Dave Kelly, Barbara Lalicki, Carrie O'Banion, Diandra Mae, P.J. Meriwether, Dianne Odegard, Lara Robertson, and, of course, my wife, Nina. A special thank-you to Google Maps and RoadsideAmerica.com.

"Sometimes we spend so much time and energy thinking about where we want to go that we don't notice where we happen to be."

—*Nobody said this. But somebody should have.*

To the Reader . . .

All the places mentioned in this book are real.

You can visit them. You *should* visit them!

Cont

Chapter 1

YOU MISSED A LOT!

There were thirteen items on Coke McDonald's To Do list on July 11th. But getting shoved into a spinning clothes dryer was not one of them.

SEND POSTCARDS HOME was on the list.

FINISH SUMMER READING was on the list.

GET A BIRTHDAY PRESENT FOR MOM was on the list.

LEARN HOW TO PLAY HARMONICA was on the list.

But nothing about getting shoved into a spinning clothes dryer.

And yet, strangely enough, getting shoved into a spinning clothes dryer was the *one* thing that Coke McDonald was actually going To Do at the middle of July.

Right now, I could tell you the amazing story of how Coke was shoved into a spinning clothes dryer. But to fully appreciate the awesomeness of it all, you should really read the first three books in The Genius Files series. So you might want to close this book for now, ask your librarian for the other books, and start reading them. I'll be waiting right here.

Don't worry, I won't let anybody else read this book until you get back.

Back so soon?

What? You say somebody *else* checked out the first three Genius Files books? How *dare* they!

Okay, tell you what I'm going to do—and I don't do this for everybody. I'll give you a quick recap of what happened up until this point. Ready?

(Deep breath)

The first book started with a pair of twins—Coke and Pepsi McDonald—jumping off a cliff near San

Francisco, California. Why would two perfectly normal twelve-year-old kids jump off a cliff? Glad you asked. They were being chased by some evil-looking dudes wearing bowler hats who were shooting poisoned darts at them with blowguns. Why were these bowler dudes trying to kill Coke and Pep? Because the eccentric Dr. Herman Warsaw told them to, that's why. And bowler dudes always do what they're told.

You see, after witnessing the attack on the Pentagon on 9/11, Dr. Warsaw started a secret government program—called The Genius Files—to have the smartest kids solve the problems of the world. But as you well know, the younger generation has this nasty habit of not doing what grown-ups tell them to do. So Dr. Warsaw decided to kill off the program, and kill off all the kids with it.

Did I mention that Dr. Warsaw is insane?

(Deep breath)

So the twins and their clueless parents set off in an RV on their cross-country summer vacation. Their dad is a history professor who's trying to come up with a killer idea for his next book. Their mom runs a popular website called *Amazing but True*, and so they had to stop off along the way at oddball tourist destinations such as the Duct Tape Capital of the World (Avon, Ohio), the Largest Frying Pan in the World

(Rose Hill, North Carolina), and the Largest Ball of Twine in the World (Cawker City, Kansas). They also visited the National Yo-Yo Museum, the Waffle House Museum, and museums devoted to Spam, Pez dispensers, and hot dog buns.

Who knew that America had such a rich cultural heritage?

(Deep breath)

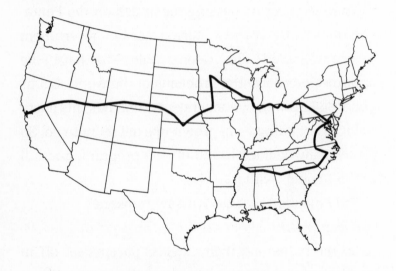

Anyway, as Coke and Pep were on the road, Dr. Warsaw and his henchman were in hot pursuit, desperately trying to—oh, how do I put this delicately?—KILL THEM. In addition to being forced to jump off a cliff, the twins got locked in their burning school, pushed into a sandpit and left to die, zapped with electric shocks, lowered into boiling oil in a giant french fry machine, run down by a remote-controlled car, and dipped in soft-serve ice cream while tied up in a Mister Softee truck.

Other than that, it was a fairly uneventful summer.

The final scene of *The Genius Files: You Only Die Twice* took place in Memphis, Tennessee. Coke and Pep were chased out of Graceland by an Elvis Presley impersonator who turned out to be (spoiler alert!) their own Aunt Judy in disguise. The twins ran away to hide in their RV, where Coke had stashed his backpack stuffed with enough fireworks to wage a small war. Evil Elvis/Aunt Judy (who happened to be a pyromaniac) accidentally lit the backpack on fire. That was the end of the RV, and that, for better or worse, was the end of Aunt Judy too.

You're probably curious to know what's going to happen next. Well, you're about to find out. So sit back, relax, and enjoy *The Genius Files: From Texas with Love*.

Chapter 2

NO MORE RUNNING

Coke McDonald looked up and saw blue sky overhead, crisscrossed by a series of wires stretching on into what appeared to be infinity. He was lying on a hard surface that seemed to be vibrating. It was windy and cold, and he couldn't move.

Of *course* he couldn't move. His legs were tied together with rope, and his wrists were shackled by handcuffs.

He saw something else too. The horrible smiling face of Dr. Herman

Warsaw leaning over him. His breath was bad.

"I had thought that you, and geniuses like you, would be able to solve the problems of the world," Dr. Warsaw told him. "That was my grand plan. But then I realized you were just like all the other kids—snotty, disrespectful, disobedient, and immoral. You killed my young assistant Archie. Then you killed my wife. And you almost killed me. So now I'm going to kill you, at last!"

Coke trembled with fear. Out of the corner of his eye, he could see he was on the roadway of a long suspension bridge. Cars and trucks were whizzing by, but none of them were stopping.

"I didn't mean to do *anything*!" Coke pleaded. "I'm just an ordinary kid. I didn't ask to be part of your stupid Genius Files program!"

"Shut up!" Dr. Warsaw hissed. "I'm finished arguing with you! This is the end of the line."

"That's right!"

The voice came from behind, and Coke realized the two bowler dudes were kneeling there, hovering over him.

"You tell 'im, boss," said the mustachioed bowler dude. His clean-shaven brother just snickered in the background.

On Coke's other side was the maniacally grinning

face of Mrs. Higgins, his health teacher.

"No more running," she said, touching the scar on her neck that she received back at The House on the Rock. "No more hiding. Finally, we have you right where we want you, and this time none of your pals are around to bail you out."

She was right. Coke looked around frantically. Mya and Bones weren't anywhere to be seen. Neither was his sister.

"Where's Pep?" Coke shouted. "Where's my sister? What did you do to her?"

"She's dead!" yelled Mrs. Higgins. "We threw her off the bridge."

"Noooooooo!" Coke screamed.

Why weren't the cars stopping? Where were the police?

"Mrs. Higgins," Dr. Warsaw said politely, "would you like the honor of sending this young man to his watery grave?"

"Oh, I'm flattered and honored that you would even consider me for such an important task," Mrs. Higgins said, smiling girlishly. "But this is your moment, Doctor. It would only be right if you did the deed yourself. The boys and I will assist you, of course."

"If you wish."

The bowler dudes grabbed Coke by his legs while

Dr. Warsaw and Mrs. Higgins hoisted him up under each arm.

Coke looked around and saw they were in the middle of the bridge. It would be a *long* way down to the water. He knew from skimming a physics textbook years earlier that for a body falling from a great height, hitting the water would be like hitting concrete. Mentally, Coke began calculating the angle and velocity his body would reach just before impact with the water. He remembered that the kinetic energy in different parts of his body was greater than the binding energy keeping them connected, so when it struck the surface his body would act more like a fluid, in the most disgusting possible way.

In simpler terms, he was about to die.

"Any last words?" Dr. Warsaw asked, interrupting Coke's train of thought.

"No!" Coke shouted. "I'll do anything you want! Anything! Just let me go!"

"Too late for negotiations," Dr. Warsaw said. "It's the real thing, Coke."

"Good one, boss," said the bowler dudes.

"Shut up!" Dr. Warsaw barked at them. "Help me throw him over this railing."

"No!" Coke protested as they swung his body backward, and then forward.

9

"One! Two!" the bowler dudes counted off.

The four of them swung Coke's body back once more, and this time they let go, heaving him over the railing and off the bridge.

He was falling.

He was helpless.

It was all over.

Chapter 3

FAMILY HUG

"**C**oke!" Pep shouted. "Wake up!"

"I don't want to die!" Coke shouted. "I don't want to die!"

"You're not gonna die!" his sister insisted.

Coke looked around. He was no longer on a bridge. He was sitting on the bench in the RV park across the street from Graceland, just as he had been before he nodded off.

"Huh? What? You're alive!"

"You must have been having a bad dream," Pep told him. "How could you *possibly* fall asleep at a time like this? You were snoring and shouting and slobbering all over me."

Coke shook his head and snapped out of it. He could see and smell the smoldering ruins of the RV, and he instantly remembered everything that had happened.

"Aunt Judy," he whispered. "She's dead."

"We killed her," Pep said, choking back tears. "I'm responsible for the death of another human being."

"She killed *herself*," Coke said quietly. "We had nothing to do with it."

It certainly wasn't their fault, but even so the twins had played a part in the accident. And it was their own aunt who was the victim. This was after they had already been involved in *another* accidental death back in Washington, when Archie Clone tried to drop them on the Washington Monument. They were beginning to think they were not entirely innocent in these tragedies. And bad news, it is said, comes in threes.

"What do you think happened to her?" Pep asked. "I mean, why did she go crazy like that?"

"Who knows?" Coke replied. "She was in love with Dr. Warsaw. I guess she would do anything for him."

The police had not arrived on the scene yet. There was nothing left of the RV, except for the charred remains of the vehicle's chassis. A crowd of gawkers had gathered around to watch it melt and take phone pictures of the carnage. This was the r exciting thing to happen around Graceland since the days when Elvis—the *real* Elvis—used to live there.

"Somebody was probably smoking in bed," a lady said.

"Coulda been a propane tank," said a man in over-alls. "I never trust them things."

Only Coke and Pep knew what really happened. Pep covered her nose to avoid inhaling the noxious fumes, and scanned the crowd. There were several suspicious-looking characters walking around, but at least none of them looked like Mrs. Higgins, Dr. War-saw, or the bowler dudes.

"What do we tell Mom and Dad?" Pep asked her brother.

"I don't know," Coke replied. "But we can't tell Mom about Aunt Judy. Knowing that her sister was an assassin would be too painful."

Soon their parents returned from their tour of Graceland.

"What's that smell?" Dr. McDonald asked Coke and Pep as he walked through the gate at the Graceland RV Park & Campground. "It smells like burning tires."

Yes—burning tires, a burning engine, a burning transmission, a burning radiator, and every other part of an RV that can burn. When Dr. and Mrs. McDonald

realized which RV it was, they stopped in their tracks.

"Honey, is that where we parked our . . . ," Mrs. McDonald said.

"I'd better call the insurance company," said Dr. McDonald.

It had been a good vehicle, all in all. It took them over four thousand miles without any problems. It never needed any serious maintenance. But now all that was left was a pile of twisted metal.

"I can't believe it," Mrs. McDonald said, stunned. She repeated it over and over again, as if that would change what had happened. "Everything's gone."

"It's all my fault," Coke admitted. "I'm really sorry."

"*You* blew up the RV?" his mother asked.

"Not exactly," Pep explained.

"It's like this," Coke said, and then he proceeded to tell his parents the whole story. He explained how they met Evil Elvis back in New Bern, North Carolina, and how The King had terrorized Pep at the Birthplace of Pepsi and almost shredded him at the World of Coca-Cola in Atlanta. He told his parents how Evil Elvis had pulled a gun on them at the grave site of Elvis, and how he chased them into the RV, grabbed the backpack filled with explosives, and accidentally ignited it and detonated the fireworks inside.

Dr. McDonald took a long look into Coke's eyes, as if he was trying to peer inside his son's soul. Mrs.

McDonald just shook her head. Coke fully expected to be grounded for the rest of his life, if not longer. He deserved it.

Instead, Dr. McDonald leaned back his head and burst out laughing.

"Oh man, that is a *great* story!" he said, clapping each of the twins on the back. "If only I had your imagination. It makes me wish I was a kid again."

"You're not mad?" Pep asked.

"Mad?" said Dr. McDonald, pulling the twins close to him. "How could I be mad at you two? It wasn't your fault. The RV must have spontaneously combusted. It had a full tank of gas. One little spark from somebody's campfire or cigarette could have set it off."

"I never trusted that thing," said Mrs. McDonald. "You read about crazy things like this happening all the time, but you just assume they'll never happen to *you*. And then, boom, it happens to you. It was just bad luck. Luckily, we paid for the insurance."

Mrs. McDonald moved in closer and threw her arms around the twins so they were in a big group hug.

"I'm just glad neither of you was inside the thing when it blew up," she said. "We're all alive, and that's what matters. Our stuff can be replaced. I don't know what I would do if something ever happened to you kids."

Coke and Pep looked at each other, and they each knew what the other one was thinking. *They* were the ones who bought all those fireworks back in South Carolina. *They* were the ones who stored them in the backpack. *They* were the ones who ran back to hide in the RV. It never would have exploded if it hadn't been for *them*. Aunt Judy would still be alive if it hadn't been for *them*. And they would have to live with that knowledge for the rest of their lives.

There was a lot that needed to be done. Mrs. McDonald, luckily, had her laptop and camera with her when the RV exploded. But everything the McDonalds had inside the RV was gone. They had no clothes, except for what they were wearing. They would have to get new toothbrushes and toiletries. Coke did a mental inventory of all the souvenirs and trinkets they had accumulated in their travels—Silly String, Frisbee, bars of soap, a harmonica, duct tape. All gone.

There were a lot of phone calls that needed to be made, police reports to fill out, statements to be given. They would have to rent a car to get back to California.

"Can we get a *cool* car this time?" Coke asked. "Like a Ferrari?"

"We're not going to rent a Ferrari," Dr. McDonald said firmly.

"Maybe we should just fly home," Pep suggested. "Then we could put this whole thing behind us."

"Fly home? No way!" her mother replied. "We said we were going to drive across the United States and back. We're almost three-quarters of the way there. It wouldn't be right to fly home now. Besides, the readers of *Amazing but True* are depending on me to send back reports."

The sun was sinking below the horizon, and most of the work that needed to be done could wait until tomorrow. For now, the immediate priority was finding somewhere to spend the night.

Fortunately, there was a nice place directly across the street from Graceland and next door to the campground—the obviously named Heartbreak Hotel.

As they walked toward it, Coke and Pep turned around to take one last look at the smoldering wreckage of the RV. Nobody could *ever* find out that Aunt Judy—disguised as Evil Elvis—had been inside.

Chapter 4
SWEET RIDE!

The Heartbreak Hotel in Memphis has an Elvis Presley theme, of course. There are pictures of Elvis all over the walls. Elvis songs blare out of hidden speakers. There's a TV in the lobby that *always* has an Elvis movie playing on it. From the looks of the place, you would never know that The King died back in 1977. It looks as though he's still alive.

Everywhere Coke and Pep turned, there were constant reminders of Evil Elvis. It made it hard to forget what happened with Aunt Judy just a few hours earlier.

Still, the twins slept soundly. It was nice to be in a regular bed for a change. After a few weeks, the RV had begun to feel like a rolling jail.

In the morning, everyone was famished. The food in the RV had been incinerated in the explosion, of course. The McDonalds came downstairs at nine o'clock and took a table in the hotel restaurant. Apart from a few lonely Elvis impersonators, the place was almost empty. A giant-screen TV on the wall was showing the young Elvis dancing with Ann-Margret in the movie *Viva Las Vegas*. The waitress took everyone's order and went to the kitchen.

"Family meeting!" Dr. McDonald announced. "I've been thinking—"

"Uh-oh," Coke muttered.

"You know I've been trying to come up with a topic for my next book," Dr. McDonald continued. "I've decided that I don't want to do an Elvis Presley biography after all."

"Good idea, Dad," Pep said, visibly relieved.

"Yeah, there are probably a *thousand* books about Elvis," Dr. McDonald told them. "I was thinking that maybe for my next book I might try a novel."

"A *novel*?!" Pep said, almost spitting out her orange juice.

"Ben," said Mrs. McDonald, "you're a respected scholar, a university professor!"

"That book about coal and the Industrial Revolution

was awesome, Dad," Coke said. "I couldn't put it down."

"See?" Mrs. McDonald said. "And you tackled an important subject. And now you want to write . . . a *novel*?"

"What, you don't think I can do it?"

"You can do anything you put your mind to," Pep told her father. "That's what you always say to us, right?"

It was obvious that Dr. McDonald's feelings had been hurt. It may have been the 21st century, but he was still insecure over the fact that his wife was more successful than he was. It didn't seem fair to him that a million people visited her silly website every day to find out about ridiculous museums, giant balls of twine, and the like.

Meanwhile, his book had been a flop. Sadly, not a lot of people care about the impact of coal on the Industrial Revolution. The book sold less than three thousand copies. He wanted to write something that *everybody* would read and talk about. He wanted to see his name on the bestseller list.

"All I need to do is write a nonfiction book and add a story to it," Dr. McDonald said. "Throw in some action. Some adventure. Some conflict. How hard could that be?"

"Do you have an idea for a novel, Dad?" Coke asked.

"No. I'm just thinking about it."

The family looked at him skeptically, and Dr. McDonald decided it would be best to drop the subject for now. He pulled out his trusty Rand McNally road atlas and opened it to the big map of the United States. Leaning over it like a general planning an invasion, he stabbed his finger at Memphis, Tennessee.

"Okay, gang, here's how we're going to get home," he said.

Dr. McDonald traced a southern route west with his finger sliding across the states of Arkansas, Oklahoma, Texas, New Mexico, and Arizona. Then they would drive up to Las Vegas in the southwestern corner of Nevada, and up through California until they got back to the San Francisco area.

The food arrived just after Mrs. McDonald opened her laptop and plugged in the starting and ending points for the trip. It would be about 2,200 miles, according to the computer, plus any detours they would make. The total travel time would be one day and eleven hours, if they drove it straight. But, of course, Mrs. McDonald had no intention of traveling all those miles without stopping off along the way.

"There are some cool things right here in Memphis," she informed the group. "The National Civil Rights Museum is at the site where Martin Luther King Jr. was assassinated. And Sun Studio is here too. That's where Elvis, Jerry Lee Lewis, Carl Perkins, and all those other singers recorded their first songs."

"I say we blow this pop stand," Coke said.

"I second that," said Pep, glancing at her brother. "It gives me the creeps."

After breakfast, the McDonalds went to the front desk to arrange for two taxis to pick them up—one for the boys and one for the girls.

Pep and her mom went to the Southland Mall, just two miles from Graceland on Elvis Presley Boulevard. They filled a couple of shopping carts with clothes, toiletries, bathing suits, and other necessities to replace what had burned in the RV. Pep took advantage of the situation to pick out a new wardrobe for herself. Like most girls her age, she was starting to care about fashion and the way she looked. She also bought a little notepad and pen that could fit in her pocket so she could jot down thoughts on the go.

Some might say it was sexist for the girls to go shopping and the boys to look at cars. But the fact is that Pep and her mother loved to shop, and Coke and his father loved cars. It was as simple as that.

The boys got into their taxi and told the driver to take them to the nearest car rental dealership. After a few minutes, the cab pulled up to a place called 4 Cheap Car Rentals.

"How about we get a Ferrari, Dad?" Coke asked, knowing full well what the answer would be.

"We've been through this," his father replied. "Mom would throw a fit if we came back with a Ferrari."

It doesn't hurt to ask.

The middle-aged salesman with a name tag that said FRANK led them out to the lot, which was filled with hundreds of vehicles. After looking over three or four dependable, four-door, family-friendly cars, Frank walked past a low-slung candy-apple-red sports car parked off to the side.

"What's *that*?" Coke asked.

"A Ferrari," Frank said. "The 612 Scaglietti. But I can't rent you that one."

"Why not?" Coke asked.

"That's *my* car. But you can sit in it if you want."

"Shotgun!" Coke called, hopping in.

Dr. McDonald slid into the driver's seat. Frank leaned in the window.

"It's a V12 engine," he said casually. "They improved the fluid dynamic characteristics of the intake and exhaust manifolds, so it can generate 540 horse-power at 7,250 rpm."

"I bet this baby can go from zero to a hundred in like five seconds!" Coke gushed.

"Four point two," Frank said.

Dr. McDonald put his hands on the steering wheel and started to feel chills running up and down his spine. He remembered the time they had stopped at the Bonneville Salt Flats back in Utah. It had been so exciting to push the accelerator all the way down to the floor and see how fast the clunky RV could go. A Ferrari would make the RV seem to drive like a glacier.

"Hand-stitched leather interior," Frank continued as he turned on the radio. "Sweet sound system. Three tweeters on the dash, two woofers and two tweeters on the sides of the rear seats, an amplified bass box in the front, and a hundred-watt subwoofer in the rear."

"You can blow your eardrums out if you want to," Coke said, as if that was a good thing. He fiddled with the knobs and techno music thumped out of the speakers. The salivary glands in Dr. McDonald's oral cavity began secreting liquid. His eyes were glazing over. He closed them.

"All-aluminum space-frame chassis," Frank said. "Aerodynamic lines. Twin xenon projector headlights. I'll tell ya, I love my wife, but this car is—"

"I want it," Dr. McDonald said.

"What?!" Coke said, a mixture of joy and alarm on his face. "But you said that Mom—"

"I never had a *cool* car before," Dr. McDonald said. "I've never even *driven* a cool car. I always bought 'practical' cars. Cars that were dependable and

reliable, and got good gas mileage. Cars that got you from point A to point B. Boring cars. But I feel like I was destined to own this automobile."

"Can't say I blame you," Frank chimed in. "It's one sweet ride."

"This car is your manifest destiny, Dad!" Coke said.

"The seat even feels like it was molded to the shape of my body," Dr. McDonald marveled.

"This is awesome," Coke said, clapping his father on the shoulder. "You are totally sticking it to The Mom."

And maybe he was. Deep inside—maybe subconsciously—he still felt some anger that his wife had just about laughed at him when he said he wanted to write a novel. Maybe he couldn't do it. Maybe he was destined to be a boring history professor for the rest of his life. But he could drive this car. He *wanted* this car. He worked hard. He deserved a car like this.

Little did Coke or Dr. McDonald know that Frank didn't actually own the Ferrari. 4 Cheap Car Rentals *always* kept a Ferrari off to the side specifically to entice men who were going through their midlife crisis. As soon as one of the Ferraris was sold, another would take its place. The lot sold more Ferraris than anything else.

"Well, like I told you, I can't rent this car," Frank said, "but if you'd be interested—"

"I'll take it," Dr. McDonald said, slapping hands with Coke.

"What about a test drive?"

"I'll *take* it."

Pep and her mother were waiting in the parking lot of the Heartbreak Hotel after getting this text from Coke: BACK IN 5 MIN WITH CAR. When they saw the Ferrari pull into the driveway, their jaws dropped open.

"I don't believe it," Pep said.

"You rented a *sports car*?" asked Mrs. McDonald.

"No, I *bought* a sports car!" her husband said proudly. "And it's not just *any* sports car, Bridge. It's a Ferrari 612 Scaglietti."

"Chicks totally dig Ferraris," said Coke excitedly. "This is a chick magnet."

"Women!" Pep yelled at him. "Not chicks! And how would *you* know what chicks dig anyway, doofus? You've never had a girlfriend."

"Don't call your brother a doofus," Mrs. McDonald said, her jaw still open.

"Can I drive this bad boy around the parking lot, Dad?" begged Coke.

"Don't even *think* about it," his father replied.

"How about when I get my license in a few years?"

"We'll talk about it in a few years."

"It's not very practical, Ben," Mrs. McDonald said, her hands on her hips.

"Yeah, I know," Dr. McDonald replied. "The RV was practical. It was so practical that it practically burned to a crisp. I figured that after what we've been through, we deserve to have a little fun. Am I right?"

"*We* deserve to have a little fun, Ben?" asked Mrs. McDonald. "Or *you* deserve to have a little fun?"

"We *all* deserve to have a little fun," he replied.

"There's hardly any luggage space," she countered.

"Perfect!" he replied. "We have hardly any luggage."

"I'm sure the gas mileage will be terrible," she argued.

"Do you know what kind of mileage the RV got?" he shot back. "Eight miles to the gallon."

In any case, the deed was done. They had essentially traded in a hulking behemoth of a recreational vehicle for a tricked-out chick magnet that was capable of going from zero to a hundred miles per hour in 4.2 seconds.

Mrs. McDonald shook her head and checked out of the hotel while Coke, Pep, and their dad loaded their stuff into the little trunk.

"Are you guys ready to blow this pop stand?" Dr.

McDonald asked when everyone was belted in.

"Yeah," Pep said. "Let's get out of here."

Dr. McDonald revved the engine, and the Ferrari came to life with a purring sound that regular old boring cars don't make.

"You hear that?" he said excitedly. "This baby wants to *run*!"

"Put the pedal to the metal, Dad!" Coke yelled.

"This is your midlife crisis, isn't it, Ben?" Mrs. McDonald asked.

"Yes!"

"Please don't go over the speed limit," she warned. "You'll get a ticket."

He revved the engine one more time, and pointed the Ferrari west.

Chapter 5

THE DIVIDING LINE

At this point, you may be starting to wonder when Coke is going to be shoved into a spinning clothes dryer. Please! Have a little patience. Our story is just beginning, and the journey has not even begun. Stick with it, dear reader, and your unhealthy thirst for blood, gore, and tragedy will be satisfied.

By the way, if you'd like to follow the McDonalds on their trip back home to California, it's easy. Get on the internet and go to Google Maps (http://maps.google.com), MapQuest (www.mapquest.com), Rand McNally (www.randmcnally.com), or whatever navigation website you like best.

Go ahead, I'll wait.

Okay, now type in 3717 Elvis Presley Boulevard, Memphis TN and click SEARCH MAPS. Click the little + or - sign on the screen to zoom in or out until you get a sense of where the twins are. Did you find Graceland? That's our starting point.

Now click Get Directions. In the A box, type Graceland, Memphis TN. In the B box, type Little Rock AR. Then click Get Directions.

Dr. McDonald made a left turn onto Elvis Presley Boulevard heading north and accelerated smoothly to merge onto I-55. He enjoyed the admiring glances he was getting from the drivers in the cars as he passed them. Especially the young female drivers.

"Keep your eyes on the road, Ben," advised Mrs. McDonald.

"This car totally kicks butt, Dad!" Coke said.

"Stick with me, pal," his father replied, pushing the gas pedal just a little farther than necessary to impress the family and feel the *vrooooom* of the Ferrari as it nosed over the speed limit.

Soon they were on I-40 and the ramp of the Hernando De Soto Bridge, with a large body of water in front of them.

"Feast your eyes, y'all," Dr. McDonald announced in a ridiculously exaggerated fake Southern accent. "Yonder lies the mighty Mississippi. The largest river system in North America. Gateway to the West. Home to Huck Finn, Lewis and Clark—"

"We *get* it, Dad."

"*Ol' man river,*" Dr. McDonald began to sing, "*dat old man river . . .*"

"Please, Dad, not that," advised Coke, with an eye roll to the left.

"*Mississippi Queeeeeeeeen!*" belted Dr. McDonald. "*If you know what I mean . . .*"

"Please stop singing, Dad," advised Pep, with an eye roll to the right.

"Do you kids know *anything* about the Mississippi River?" asked Mrs. McDonald. She, of course, knew that her son had a photographic memory and recalled just about everything he had ever seen, read, heard, smelled, or tasted.

"The name Mississippi comes from the Ojibwe Indians," Coke informed the others. "They called the river Misi-zibi, which means 'Father of Waters.'"

"Here we go again," Pep muttered, clearly annoyed.

It's not easy living with somebody who has total recall, and especially when he's your twin brother. Pep's teachers always seemed a little disappointed that she didn't have her brother's incredible ability to remember information.

Coke had read about the Ojibwe Indians on the back of a cereal box five years earlier, and couldn't resist sharing the information.

"You probably know that a raindrop falling into Lake Itasca in Minnesota will travel the length of the Mississippi and arrive at the Gulf of Mexico about

33

ninety days later," he said.

Now he was just showing off.

"Thank you, Mr. Boring!" Pep muttered, unable to restrain herself. "You probably just made that up."

There was still a long way to go before the McDonald family would be home, but the Mississippi River seemed like a sort of symbolic dividing line between east and west. Pep turned around to glance out the back window and see the Memphis skyline getting smaller in the distance. They were finally on their way back to California. Like the Memphis skyline, their troubles seemed to be fading from view.

As soon as they crossed the Hernando De Soto Bridge, this sign appeared at the side of the highway:

"Woo-hoo!" Coke shouted. "Arkansas! The Natural State! The birthplace of Walmart! Did you know that in Arkansas it's against the law to push a live moose out of a moving plane? That's a fact!"

"Ah reckon I won't be pushin' no live mooses outta no air-o-planes then, pardner," said Dr. McDonald.

"That accent is lame, Dad," Coke remarked.

"It's also insulting to the good people of Arkansas," said Mrs. McDonald. "They don't speak like that."

"Then ah reckon ah better shut mah cakehole," her husband replied. "Don't wanna get no Arkansasians all riled up or nothin'."

"So I guess there's some weird Arkansas museum or tacky tourist trap you'll be taking us to," said Coke, to change the subject. "Maybe the largest peanut in the world?"

"No, that's in Oklahoma," Mrs. McDonald said as she picked up her Arkansas travel guide, which was conveniently titled *Arkansas Travel Guide*. "But they do have the world's largest wind chimes, in Eureka Springs. Hmmm, let's see. The town of Alma, Arkansas, calls itself the Spinach Capital of the World. In Mountain View, they have their Annual Bean Fest and Outhouse Races. And once a year in Yellville, they have a turkey drop. They toss live turkeys out of airplanes. That would be pretty interesting to see, don't

you think? But Yellville is pretty far north of here."

"There's just so much to see and do in Arkansas," Pep said sarcastically. "How will we ever decide?"

"How about we let Dad decide for a change?" suggested Mrs. McDonald.

"Y'know, after what we've been through with the RV, I just want to *relax*," said Dr. McDonald. "Is there a nice place in Arkansas where we can go and just kick back for a day? Maybe do a little swimming or water sports?"

"Yes!" shouted Mrs. McDonald, as she looked through the book. "Hot Springs! It's two and a half hours from here, and west."

"Yee-ha!" Dr. McDonald exclaimed. "Ah reckon I'm fit to be tied after falling in the hog wallow!"

"That doesn't even mean anything, Dad," Pep said.

Everyone was laughing and having a fun old time. The kids would never forget what had happened to Aunt Judy in Memphis, of course. But for the moment, she was not on their minds.

Mrs. McDonald was punching "Hot Springs, Arkansas" into the GPS when her cell phone rang.

"Hello?" she said. "Oh, hi! Nice to hear from you. How are you doing? What?! For *how* long? Are you joking? No, I have no idea. Okay, thanks."

When she hung up, she had a worried look on her face.

"Who was that?" everybody asked.

"It was Hermy," Mrs. McDonald told them. "You know, my sister's new husband, Dr. Herman Warsaw. He said Judy is missing. He hasn't seen her in a couple of days. Gee, I hope she's okay."

"I thought they were on their honeymoon," said Dr. McDonald. "Where could she be?"

Coke and Pep looked at each other. They knew exactly where Aunt Judy was. Or what was left of her, anyway.

Chapter 6

TALKING WITH STRANGERS

In the backseat, Coke and Pep sat stunned and silent. On the inside, the twins both knew the right thing to do—come clean and tell their parents what had happened to Aunt Judy in the RV. But they couldn't bring themselves to do it.

How do you break the news to your mother that her sister was a psychopath and pyromaniac who tried to kill you? How do you tell her that her sister blew herself up? It's impossible. Besides, every time the twins tried to be honest and tell their parents the truth, they didn't believe it.

Coke and Pep kept their mouths shut. What happened to Aunt Judy in the RV would be their secret, at least for the time being.

Awkward silence filled the car as the Ferrari headed west through Arkansas, passing Dagmar State Wildlife Management Area and Wattensaw State Game Area. Unless you were a nature lover, there wasn't a whole lot to look at outside the window.

"Hey, let's play the spy game!" Dr. McDonald blurted out enthusiastically.

Groans came out of the backseat.

"Come on, it'll be fun!" he said. "See if you can find the letters of the alphabet outside the car. I'll start. Look! The *A* for 'Arkansas' is on that license plate right in front of us."

"*B*," said Mrs. McDonald. "The sign on that building to the right."

"*C*," Dr. McDonald said. "On that billboard. How about one of you kids take a turn?"

"We don't want to play, Dad," Pep replied.

"You kids are no fun at all," he said.

The game ended right there. The twins went back to their private thoughts. As the Ferrari cruised west along I-40, signs started to appear for Little Rock, the state capital.

39

"I wonder why it's called Little Rock?" asked Dr. McDonald.

"They probably have a bunch of little rocks," Pep guessed.

"Actually, Little Rock gets its name from a rock formation on the south bank of the Arkansas River," Coke informed the rest of the family. "It was called 'la Petite Roche,' which means 'the little rock' in French. I saw that—"

"Shut up!" Pep shouted at her brother. "Nobody cares!"

"Don't tell your brother to shut up," Dr. McDonald told Pep. "It's not his fault that he knows a lot of things."

"I can't take it anymore!" Pep shouted. She picked up a magazine and whacked Coke on the shoulder with it.

"Ow! Knock it off!"

At this point, Dr. McDonald made an executive decision. Everyone's nerves suddenly seemed to be on edge. The stress of seeing the RV explode had clearly gotten to Pep. Everybody needed to calm down a little.

"I'm starved," he said as he pulled off the highway at the Little Rock exit and crossed the Arkansas River.

One block off the riverbank was a bustling street

with a convention center, the Little Rock River Market, and some restaurants.

"How about this joint?" Mrs. McDonald said as they approached a place called Flying Fish.

Dr. McDonald pulled into the parking lot. Flying Fish, needless to say, specializes in seafood. The family slid into a booth and ordered an assortment of catfish, shrimp, oysters, crab, and gumbo for everyone to share.

"You think they have grits?" Coke asked. "I always wanted to try grits."

"Grits sound gross," Pep said.

"Well, you don't listen to them," Coke told his sister. "You eat them."

One wall of the restaurant was an unusual sight—row upon row of wooden plaques, each one with a fish mounted on it. There were more than three hundred of them, and all of them looked the same. Upon closer examination, it was obvious that the fish were made out of rubber. At the top of the wall was a sign: BILLY BASS ADOPTION CENTER.

"What the heck?" Coke asked.

"This will be great for *Amazing but True!*" Mrs. McDonald said as she grabbed her camera.

Dr. McDonald explained to the kids that, around the turn of the century, millions of people bought

these silly novelty gifts called Big Mouth Billy Bass. The head and the tail of the fish would wiggle back and forth while the fish sang songs like "Don't Worry, Be Happy" and "Take Me to the River." The fish's mouth even moved while it sang.

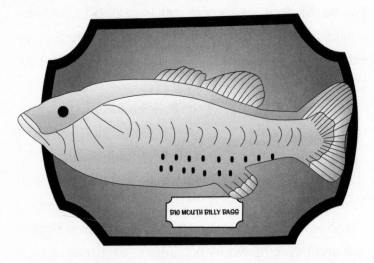

Don't believe me? YouTube it. Go ahead, I'll wait.

Anyway, Big Mouth Billy Bass was really annoying, and when the fad ended, people were stuck with the silly toys. A lot of the fish ended up in the garbage or at garage sales. Some of them, apparently, ended up at Flying Fish Restaurant in Little Rock, Arkansas.

"Do you like our little museum?" asked the waitress when she brought the food. "If you donate a Big Mouth Billy Bass to our collection, you get a free catfish basket."

Mrs. McDonald took notes for her website. She seemed to have an uncanny knack for stumbling upon the kind of oddball tourist spots that don't appear in any guidebooks.

As they were finishing their food, a couple of flannel-shirted, heavyset, bearded truckers slid into the booth next to them. Dr. McDonald and Mrs. McDonald went to pay the check while Coke and Pep eavesdropped on the truckers' conversation.

"So I was comin' in loud and proud, doing the double nickel on I-95 when this meat wagon on my left hit the mix-master," said the first trucker.

"What did you do?" asked the other trucker.

"Well, I backed off the hammer," he replied. "So this wiggle wagon was in the granny lane and wearing my bumper out. So I put the pedal to the metal and the next thing I know, there's a bear in the air. And that's how I ended up here at the Pickle Park."

"Looks like you're gonna need a dragon wagon," said the first trucker.

"Reckon so. Catch ya on the flip-flop."

Coke and Pep had no idea what the truckers were talking about, but they were mesmerized by them.

"*Pssssst!* Hey, kids," the first trucker suddenly whispered.

"I'm sorry, but we don't talk to strangers," Pep informed him.

The second trucker winked and carefully peeled off the corner of his beard. Or, I should say, *her* beard. Because he was a she.

"Mya!" exclaimed Pep.

"Bones!" exclaimed Coke. "Nice disguises!"

"Shhhhh!" whispered Mya. "You'll blow our cover."

Now, if you've been following The Genius Files books, you know who Bones and Mya are. They are kindly grown-ups who once worked for Dr. Warsaw to start The Genius Files project, but quit when he lost his mind and became determined to kill off all the children. At that point, Bones and Mya made it their mission to help Coke, Pep, and any other Genius Filers who were being pursued by Dr. Warsaw and his evil henchman. They had already saved the twins' lives several times.

"What are *you* doing here?" Pep asked as she hugged them. "And why are you dressed up like truckers?"

"We heard about the good work you did at Graceland," said Mya. "The way you took out Evil Elvis was beautiful. It was almost like a work of art."

"It was an accident," Coke told them. "We didn't mean for that to happen. We were just running away. Trying to stay alive."

"She was our aunt," Pep said. "I mean, we hardly knew her, but even so. How could it have happened? She was just a normal person, and then she turned into this . . . monster."

"It happens," Bones told them. "Monsters aren't born that way. They start out as cute babies, like everybody else. And then, somewhere along the line, they change. Maybe it's genetic. Maybe it's their environment. Sometimes perfectly normal people snap and go crazy and we never find out the reason why."

"What's done is done," Mya said philosophically. "All that matters now is that the monster is dead. Evil Elvis will never hurt you, or anyone else, again."

"What did you tell your parents about it?" asked Bones.

"Nothing," Coke replied.

"Good," Bones said. "It would be best for them not to be involved. They would call the police, and that would just open up a big can of worms."

"What are we supposed to do *now*?" Pep asked. "Dr. Warsaw called on my mom's cell phone. He said Aunt Judy was missing and he wanted to know if our folks knew where she was."

"I'm not worried about Warsaw," said Mya. "He sent Archie Clone after you, and we know what happened

to him. Then he sent Aunt Judy after you, and we know what happened to her. Dr. Warsaw may be mentally unstable, but he isn't dumb. By now he must realize that playing with you is playing with fire—literally. He'll probably go crawl back into the little hole where he came from. You'll never have to worry about him again."

"That would be a big relief," Pep said.

"You probably won't be seeing us anymore," Bones told the twins. "So we got you a little something. Sort of a going-away present."

He opened a bag on the table.

"Oh, you don't have to give us presents!" Pep said.

"Is it a Frisbee grenade?" Coke asked hopefully. "We can definitely use another one of those."

Bones pulled out a small, thin metal object with five little prongs at the end. It sort of telescoped open, like the antenna of a portable radio. He handed it to the twins.

"You got us . . . a backscratcher?" asked Pep.

"It's not a backscratcher, you dope!" Coke told his sister. "It's obviously a blowgun *disguised* as a backscratcher, right? You blow into one end and it shoots out poisoned darts that will paralyze somebody in seconds. That is cool!"

"Uh, it's not a blowgun," Bones said.

"No?" said Coke. "I know! It's like one of those stun gun things. You push a little button hidden in the handle and it shoots out sixty thousand volts of electricity. *Bzzzzzzt!* That'll give a bad guy something to think about! Thanks! This could really come in handy."

"It's not a stun gun," Mya said. "It's a—"

"How could I have been so dumb?" asked Coke. "I know. You break off a piece of the backscratcher and put it into somebody's drink, right? It dissolves, and the next thing they know they're coughing up blood and begging you to give them the antidote. Right?"

"Wrong."

"There's no antidote for the poison?" Coke asked.

"There's no poison, and there's no antidote," said Bones. "You must understand, we have no budget for high-tech—"

"Maybe you can stab somebody with this thing?" Coke asked hopefully.

"It's a *backscratcher*," insisted Mya, demonstrating it. "That's *all* it is. You use it to scratch your back! You know, in those hard-to-reach places. It telescopes. See?"

Go to Google Maps
(http://maps.google.com).

Click Get Directions.

In the A box, type
Little Rock AR.

In the B box, type
Bauxite AR.

Click Get Directions.

"We don't need a backscratcher!" Coke said, disappointed. "We need something we can use to defend ourselves from the crazy people who are trying to kill us!"

"Look," Bones said. "You've got to believe me. Nobody is trying to kill you anymore. Relax! Enjoy the rest of your vacation. The coast is clear."

The coast may have been clear. It was Arkansas, Texas, Arizona, and New Mexico that the twins were worried about.

Chapter 7

RETURN OF AN OLD FRIEND

Their tummies filled, the McDonald family was on the road again. In fact, Dr. McDonald began to sing, much to everyone's dismay, Willie Nelson's signature song "On the Road Again." As a singer, Dr. McDonald made a good history professor.

The twins stared out the window as Arkansas rolled by. They were both thinking the same thing—what if Bones and Mya were *wrong*? What if the coast *wasn't* clear? What if Mrs. Higgins or those pesky bowler dudes were waiting for them at their next stop, ready to leap out and do some horribly unspeakable thing? Or what if there was a *new* threat out there waiting to attack them?

Coke made a mental note to never let down his guard.

On the first half of their journey, most of the highway signs had an *E*, for east, after the route number. Now the highway signs ended in a *W*. The McDonalds were on their way home.

"Hot Springs, here we come!" Dr. McDonald bellowed as he merged onto I-30 West out of Little Rock. Mrs. McDonald opened her Arkansas guidebook and casually leafed through it. They had only traveled about fourteen miles when they approached exit 123—Bryant/Bauxite.

"Ben, stop the car!" Mrs. McDonald shouted suddenly.

He swerved off to the shoulder of the road and slammed on the brakes, nearly causing an accident and frightening the other drivers. The Ferrari screeched to a halt. Books, maps, papers, pens, and anything else that wasn't held down went flying into the front seat. Had they not been wearing seat belts, the whole family would have gone through the windshield.

"What's wrong?" Dr. McDonald asked, his heart racing. "Did I hit something?"

"This is the exit for Bauxite, Arkansas!" Mrs. McDonald said excitedly.

"So?" replied the rest of the family.

"The town is named after bauxite!"

A moment of silence.

"What's bauxite?" asked Pep.

"It's an off-white, grayish, brown, yellow, or reddish-brown rock," Coke informed her. "They make aluminum out of it."

He remembered that from a game of Trivial Pursuit he had played years ago.

"Thank you, Mr. Wikipedia," Pep said, rolling her eyes.

"Don't tell me, let me guess," Dr. McDonald said. "There's a museum here—"

"Yes!" Mrs. McDonald said gleefully. "Bauxite, Arkansas, calls itself the Aluminum Capital of the World! This will be great for *Amazing but True*. And the town is just a few miles from here!"

A collective groan could be heard from inside the Ferrari.

"You know, Mom," Pep said, choosing her words carefully, "there's no rule that says we have to go to *every* capital of the world."

"That's right, Mom," Coke pointed out. "Maybe we ought to skip this one. It doesn't sound that interesting."

Dr. McDonald kept his mouth shut. He'd decided to let the kids take the heat this time.

Mrs. McDonald turned to face the backseat. Never a good sign.

"Sixty years from now, you're going to be old," she told the kids. "You're going to think back on all the things you did during your life. You'll have some regrets. We all do. And if we don't visit Bauxite, Arkansas, right now, you're going to regret that you were just a few lousy miles from the Aluminum Capital of the World and couldn't be bothered to check it out. How will you feel?"

In their heads, Coke and Pep came up with several snarky comments, along the lines of "We'll feel great!" In reality, they didn't say a word. There was no use arguing with Bridget McDonald. There was no use complaining. They would be going to Bauxite, Arkansas—the Aluminum Capital of the World.

Dr. McDonald grudgingly pulled off at the exit.

"I hope this place is more interesting than the Duct Tape Capital of the World," Coke whispered to his sister in the backseat.

Perhaps you recall, dear reader, that a similar situation occurred in *The Genius Files: Never Say Genius*. On their way to the Rock and Roll Hall of Fame, the McDonalds stumbled upon the town of Avon, Ohio, where there is an annual duct tape parade, with duct tape sculptures, a duct tape fashion show, and a dancing mascot called Duct Tape Duck.

Bauxite looked pretty much like any other small town in America. A sign said the population of the town was 432.

"They should call this place Snoozeville, USA," Coke grumbled as he looked out the window.

"The Aluminum Capital of the World?" Pep asked. "It's not like the houses here are made out of aluminum or anything."

Dr. McDonald drove past the local post office and turned south on School Street. After a few blocks, he double-parked in front of the Bauxite Museum—a colonial-style building with five columns in the front.

"You kids run inside and get tickets," said Mrs. McDonald. "We'll find a parking spot."

"Yeah, there might be a long line to get in to see the aluminum," Coke said with a smirk as he got out of the car.

"I can't believe they have a museum devoted to a *rock*," Pep told her brother as she yanked open the heavy front door.

"Why not?" Coke replied. "We've already been to museums devoted to Spam, mustard, yo-yos, Pez dispensers, vacuum cleaners, hot dog buns—"

Coke could have listed every oddball museum they had visited on the trip, but the words stuck in his throat as he gasped at the sight of someone he had hoped he would never see again.

Mrs. Higgins.

"Well, if it isn't the McDonald twins!" she said cheerfully. "Welcome to The Bauxite Museum! Fancy meeting *you* two here! I'll be your tour guide today."

"Ahhhhhhh!"

Pep nearly fainted, but her brother grabbed her before she could hit the ground.

If you've been following The Genius Files series, you're well aware that Mrs. Higgins is the germaphobic and psychotic health teacher who set the twins' school on fire while they were locked in the detention room. She also chased them through The House on the Rock in Wisconsin, forced them to cause a riot at Wrigley Field in Chicago, and tried to blow their eardrums out with heavy metal music at the Rock and Roll Hall of Fame in Cleveland.

In all fairness, Coke and Pep had not exactly reciprocated with kindness toward Mrs. Higgins. In fact, back in Kansas they had emptied the RV's toilet on her head as she sat in a convertible. And Mrs. Higgins still had a scar across her neck from the time they clothes-lined her with a ball of twine.

The twins took a terrified step backward, but the door to the museum had already closed behind them.

"Don't you dare touch us!" Coke shouted, pointing his finger at Mrs. Higgins as he leaped into one of his karate poses.

"I have no intention of touching you," she replied, still smiling cheerfully. "I'm just happy to see you again."

"Our parents will be here any second!" yelled Pep, trying to appear threatening.

"Great!" said Mrs. Higgins. "I was so disappointed that I didn't get the chance to meet them on Back-to-School Night."

"You're crazy!" Coke declared, looking around desperately for help, or at least an EXIT sign. "And you're stalking us!"

"Who, me?" asked Mrs. Higgins innocently. "Oh dear no."

"If you're not stalking us, how come you always manage to get a job wherever we happen to be?" asked Pep.

"It's just an amazing coincidence, I suppose," she replied, with a smile. "Teachers don't get paid much. I needed to earn some money over summer vacation, and here I am."

The door opened once again, and Dr. and Mrs. McDonald entered the Bauxite Museum. Coke and Pep let out a sigh of relief. That lunatic Mrs. Higgins wouldn't *dare* try anything with their parents standing right there.

It should be noted that the logical thing for the twins to do at this point would be to tell their parents all the horrible things Mrs. Higgins had done to them. By all rights, the police should be called. Mrs. Higgins should be arrested and locked up in a place where she would be in no position to harm innocent children.

But Coke and Pep didn't say a word. Their parents had never believed them before, and there was no reason to think the situation would be any different this time. The kindly looking, smiling woman in front of them seemed incapable of hurting a fly.

"Welcome to the Bauxite Museum!" said Mrs. Higgins, reaching out to shake hands with the parents. "I don't believe we've met. I'm Audrey Higgins. I had the pleasure of teaching health to your lovely children this past year. It is so nice to meet you in person."

The McDonalds made the usual adult pleasantries, mainly focusing on the difference in weather between California and Arkansas.

"Wasn't it horrible, what happened to the school?" Mrs. McDonald asked.

"Oh yes, what a tragedy," replied Mrs. Higgins.

"Did they ever find out what caused the fire?" asked Dr. McDonald.

"It's a mystery," said Mrs. Higgins, sincerity oozing from her voice.

Coke and Pep stood there, open-mouthed. Mrs. Higgins was the one who burned the school down! That was after she had locked them in the detention room! It was all her doing! She was either a fantastic liar or, more likely, insane.

"Well, thank goodness they're rebuilding the school," Mrs. McDonald said. "I received an email from a friend of mine who said it should be finished by the time the kids go back to school in September."

"That's wonderful news!" Mrs. Higgins replied.

After a few more minutes of chitchat, Mrs. Higgins led the family into the museum, taking Coke and Pep by the hand. The kids tried to pull away, but she had an iron grip.

"Let me show you around," she said. "Did you know that bauxite is the most abundant metal element in the earth's crust?"

"I *did* know that, actually," Coke replied. "It's also the state rock of Arkansas."

Mrs. Higgins spent several minutes telling the family the history of bauxite, which wasn't nearly as boring as one might expect.

"Aluminum is very light, strong, and resistant to corrosion," said Mrs. Higgins as she led them through a room filled with dusty display cases, photos, and primitive mining equipment from a century ago. "It was used to make thousands of American bombers and fighter planes during World War Two."

"Think of it," Mrs. McDonald said. "If not for bauxite, Hitler might have won the war."

"Yeah," agreed Dr. McDonald, "if not for bauxite, we'd probably be speaking German right now."

"Ich spreche Deutsch jetzt," said Coke.

"Since when do you speak German?" asked Pep.

"Since Tuesday."

"You sure know a lot about aluminum, Mrs.

Higgins," said Mrs. McDonald as she snapped photos for *Amazing but True.*

"Well, that's my job," Mrs. Higgins replied. "Come, let me show you our most popular exhibit."

She led the family to a display case labeled BAUXITE TEETH. Behind the glass were a bunch of teeth that were discolored and streaked with brown.

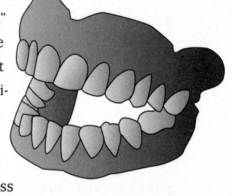

"The bauxite in the local water supply caused this," she explained. "But the funny thing is, they brought in some dentists to investigate, and they found that people with bauxite teeth had harder enamel than average, and they had less tooth decay. That's one of the reasons they started putting fluoride into toothpaste and water."

"Hmm," said Dr. McDonald. Having spent five years working on his scholarly book *The Impact of Coal on the Industrial Revolution*, he was intensely interested in minerals.

It didn't take long to see everything in the little museum. When the tour was finished, Mrs. Higgins led the family back to the front door.

"This was fascinating," said Mrs. McDonald. "Thank

you so much for the tour. My children certainly are lucky to have such a wonderful teacher."

"Yeah," Pep said. "Really lucky."

"We'll go get the car," said Dr. McDonald. "You kids can look in the gift shop."

"No!" Coke shouted. "We don't want to look in the gift shop!"

"We're coming with you!" shouted Pep, clinging to her mother like a three-year-old.

The last thing the twins wanted was to be left alone for one more minute with a psychotic killer.

"Don't be silly," their father told them. "You kids talk with Mrs. Higgins. "I'm sure you have a lot of catching up to do."

The door slammed shut as the parents left. The twins turned around, fearing the worst. Mrs. Higgins still had a sickly sweet smile on her face. She also had her hands behind her back.

"She's got a gun!" Pep yelled as she dove out of the way. "Duck!"

"No, it's a knife!" Coke shouted, covering his face with his hands.

Mrs. Higgins laughed.

"It's nothing of the sort," she assured the twins. "I wanted to give you a little present."

"Whatever it is, we don't want it," Coke told her.

"Yeah, after everything you've done to us, we don't trust you for a second," said Pep.

"Look, I want to be honest," Mrs. Higgins said. "There's a reason I'm being so nice to you."

"What is it?" asked Pep.

"I know what you did to your aunt Judy," Mrs. Higgins replied.

"We didn't do *anything* to her," Pep insisted. The thought of what happened to Aunt Judy almost brought tears to her eyes.

"Oh *please*," Mrs. Higgins said. "People don't just vanish into thin air. I'm guessing that she was in your RV when it exploded. Am I right? I just wanted to thank you for getting rid of her."

"Why?" asked Pep.

Tears welled up in Mrs. Higgins's eyes.

"You cleared the way for me," she said. "Now that Dr. Warsaw is single again, he can marry *me*. Thank you for killing her."

"We didn't kill her!" Coke said, raising his voice.

"He's the only man I've ever loved," Mrs. Higgins said softly, "and now he will be all mine. But Herman is very fragile, both physically and psychologically. He just lost his wife. He needs me to make him well again. I owe it all to you kids. Please trust me. Here's a little something to show my appreciation."

She opened her hands to reveal two chunks of bauxite, each about the size of a golf ball.

"It's a trap!" Coke warned. "Don't take it, Pep!"

"It's just a little souvenir to help you remember your visit to our museum," Mrs. Higgins said.

"They're bombs!" Coke shouted, slapping the rocks out of Mrs. Higgins's hands. "Run for it!"

He grabbed Pep's hand and together they ran out of there as fast as their feet could carry them.

Go to Google Maps (http://maps.google.com).

Click Get Directions.

In the A box, type Bauxite AR.

In the B box, type Hot Springs AR.

Click Get Directions

Chapter 8

HEAVEN IN HOT SPRINGS

Heading west out of Bauxite, Dr. McDonald eased the Ferrari onto Route 70. It's a quiet rural road, and the scenery didn't capture the kids' interest. Coke pulled out a copy of *The New England Journal of Medicine* he had found in the lobby of the Heartbreak Hotel. He started going through it like a scanner goes through pages of documents.

There wasn't a whole lot of time to pass. Forty minutes from Bauxite, signs of civilization started to appear at the side of the road. Billboards, buildings, businesses. Soon they had reached the town limits of

Hot Springs, Arkansas, nestled within the low-lying Ouachita Mountains.

It was getting late, and Dr. McDonald had driven almost two hundred miles since leaving Memphis that morning. He pulled into the first name-brand hotel he saw—a Best Western—and the family had a relaxing dinner at Outback Steakhouse.

There was a rack of travel brochures near the cash register, and the twins grabbed some of them to look through while they waited for their food. Hot Springs, they were surprised to discover, had a wax museum, a go-kart track, mini golf, a water park, an alligator farm, and the world's only diamond-producing mine that is open to the public.

"Hey, this place looks cool," Coke told the group.

"Check it out, Mom," Pep said. "The Gangster Museum of America is right here. It's a museum all about mobsters and criminals. That would be great for *Amazing but True*."

And it would be. But the McDonalds, for a change, hadn't come to Hot Springs to visit the usual tacky roadside attractions. They'd come for the *water*. First thing in the morning, the family piled into the Ferrari and found their way to a small section of town called Bathhouse Row.

"Do you kids know why this town is called Hot

Springs?" Mrs. McDonald asked the kids.

"Because spring is really hot here?" Pep quickly guessed, trying to beat her brother to the punch.

"What a dope!" Coke said, shaking his head in amazement.

"Don't call your sister a dope," scolded Dr. McDonald.

"A million gallons of natural mineral water a day flows from forty-seven springs nearby," Coke said, recalling a library book he'd once glanced at in second grade. "The water bubbles down beneath the earth to superheated areas deep in the crust, and when it gets to the surface, it's 147 degrees Fahrenheit."

"That's right!" Mrs. McDonald said.

"In fact," Coke continued, "according to scientists, the water that reaches the surface in Hot Springs today fell as rainfall four thousand years ago."

"Just shut up already, okay?"

"Don't tell your brother to shut up," warned Dr. McDonald.

"Yeah," Coke said. "Don't tell me to shut up. It's not my fault that you don't know anything."

"Shut up!"

Dr. McDonald parked the car outside a Spanish Colonial Revival building with a large dome covered by tiles.

"We're going to take a *bath*?" Pep asked warily.

In fact, taking a bath was exactly what they were going to do. Before they got out of the car, Mrs. McDonald read a section from her Arkansas guidebook:

"Hot Springs is sometimes known as Spa City. According to legend, back in the 18th century the Quapaw Indians discovered the magical healing powers of the springs. Today, millions of people pay good money to sit naked—"

"I'm not getting naked in front of a million strangers!" Pep yelled.

"You don't have to get naked," assured her mother. "I brought our bathing suits."

The guidebook went on to explain that, over the years, presidents, outlaws, movie stars, and athletes had flocked to Hot Springs to soak in the natural mineral pools. The Pittsburgh Pirates, Chicago Cubs, and Boston Red Sox used to hold their spring training camps there. Visitors would spot Babe Ruth walking down the street, sitting next to them in a tub, or gambling at the racetrack nearby. Nowadays, regular people come from all over the world to relax in the waters and ease the pain of arthritis, bursitis, rheumatic fever, and other ailments.

"I don't have any of those diseases," Pep said. "Can I wait in the car?"

"Don't be silly," Dr. McDonald said. "This is a *family* vacation. We're doing this as a family. You're going to love it."

Bathhouse Row consists of eight historic buildings and is part of Hot Springs National Park. The McDonalds climbed the steps of the Quapaw, which was built in 1922. The twins examined the Native American artwork and artifacts that decorated the lobby.

"Welcome to the Quapaw!" said the smiling lady behind the counter.

Dr. and Mrs. McDonald looked over the menu of services, which included everything from whirlpools and sitz baths to facials, foot scrubs, needle showers, aromatherapy, and hot towel wraps.

"Ooh, look, Bridge," Dr. McDonald said excitedly,

"they have Swedish massage. Your birthday is the day after tomorrow. How about a massage for a present?"

"I think I'm going to get the Invigorating Body Polish and a Moisturizing Hand Paraffin Wax Dip instead," Mrs. McDonald replied.

Quapaw Baths & Spa is sort of like an amusement park for middle-aged parents.

"Hey, how about we get a couples massage?" suggested Dr. McDonald, pulling out his credit card.

"Ewww, gross," the twins said simultaneously.

The whole idea of sitting in mineral water gave Coke and Pep the creeps, and they made no effort to pretend otherwise.

"I wish you kids would get into the spirit," their mother told them. "This is going to be a once-in-a-lifetime experience."

"Let's hope so," Coke muttered.

"That aluminum museum was a once-in-a-lifetime experience too," said Pep. "I never want to go back there again."

"Just so you know," said the lady behind the desk, "children under the age of fourteen are not allowed in the vapor cabinets."

"Vapor cabinets?" Pep said, wrinkling up her nose. She didn't want to know what a vapor cabinet was. It sounded gross.

The lady gave out robes, slippers, and locker keys, and the McDonalds went to change into their bathing suits.

Four large European-style soaking pools, each of them a different temperature, were located on the first floor. Dr. McDonald picked the hottest one and the rest of the family followed him to the edge of the pool.

"Ahhhhhh," he said as he eased himself into the water. "Oh yeah . . ."

Mrs. McDonald was the next one in. Once submerged, she closed her eyes and leaned her head back.

"Oooh, I feel my stress just melting away," she said.

Coke and Pep looked at each other. *Stress?* What stress did their mother have to deal with? *She* didn't have to jump off a cliff wearing a wingsuit. *She* wasn't thrown into a vat of Spam. *She* wasn't attacked by a remote-controlled car. *She* wasn't tied to a chair and left to die in a Mister Softee truck. *She* didn't have a band of lunatics chasing her across the country. If anybody needed to have their stress melt away, it was Coke and Pep.

And they did. As soon as they lowered themselves into the hot mineral water, they felt like they had stepped into a calmer, more peaceful world.

"Ooooooh!"

"Ahhhhhh!"

A gentle waterfall flowed on one side of the pool, and after a good long soak, Coke went over to stand under it and let the spray tumble all over his head and shoulders.

For the others, the soothing sound of the waterfall combined with the quiet music and the outdoorsy smell of the tropical plants scattered around was enough. For a few minutes, nobody wanted to speak and risk spoiling the mood.

Pep felt her anxiety slipping away. Temporarily, she was able to forget all the bad things that had happened to her since the start of summer vacation.

"This is so relaxing," Dr. McDonald finally said, breaking the silence. "I don't even remember what day of the week it is."

"I don't even remember what *month* it is," said Pep.

"Who even cares what *year* it is?" Coke said. "Just lie back and enjoy it."

After about ten minutes of this euphoria, a heavyset woman came over to the pool with towels and ice water.

"Mr. and Mrs. McDonald?" she said. "It's time for your couples massage."

"Ewww," said the twins.

"You kids enjoy yourselves," Dr. McDonald said as he stepped out of the pool and sipped from a cup of ice water. "We'll see you in about an hour."

The parents went off for their massage, while Coke and Pep continued to soak in the good vibes of the pool. But soon, when their fingertips were getting pruny, the twins decided it would be wise to get out of the water and walk around the place.

The Quapaw has several floors and lots of rooms. With no grown-ups around to tell them "You can't go in there," Coke and Pep went on a mission of exploration.

When they were little, the twins had mastered the art of "sneaking around" the hallways of a hotel late at night. This consisted of slinking around while pretending to be secret agents on a dangerous mission to find the imaginary microfilm that had been locked in one of the rooms. You had to be very quiet and hug the walls to make sure that evil ninjas—or at least the hotel security guards—would not see you with their hidden surveillance cameras and night-vision goggles.

After a few minutes of sneaking around, Coke turned a doorknob and entered a room that had two large metal boxes in it. The boxes looked a little bit like washing machines, but clearly weren't. There

was a basketball-sized hole in the top of each box.

"Look at those things," Pep said. "What do you think they are?"

"They're probably those vapor cabinets the lady was telling us about," Coke guessed. "They're like personal steam baths. They look cool. Let's try 'em!"

"We're not allowed, remember?" Pep replied. "You have to be fourteen."

"Oh, come on," Coke urged his sister. "These things must be pretty great if they won't let kids use them. What are we gonna do, melt?"

"I don't want to get in trouble," Pep argued.

"You won't get in trouble!" Coke said as he opened the door of the vapor cabinet on the left. "Look, we'll be fourteen in less than a year. Mom and Dad paid a lot of money to get us in here. Have a little fun for once in your life."

Coke climbed into one of the vapor cabinets, pulling the stainless steel door down and popping his head through the hole on the top.

Hesitantly, Pep did the same, climbing into the other vapor cabinet and sitting on a little bench inside it. The twins looked a little bit like a pair of turtles in their shells.

Below, hot water created steam, which rose up through the vapor cabinet and was trapped inside.

"This is awesome," Coke said. "Do you feel it?"

"I think I feel my pores opening—"

At that moment the lights flickered and went out.

"Oh, great," Coke said. "A power failure."

As they sat in total darkness, the twins heard rustling sounds, and then the clicking of locks. Someone was just a few feet away, moving around the room.

"Who's that?"

"I don't know."

"Coke, I have a bad feeling about this."

When the lights went back on, the twins were confronted by the most evil, the most hated, the most horrifying sight imaginable.

Dr. Herman Warsaw.

"Ahhhhhhhhhhhh!"

The twins shrank back in terror at the sight of his face. Despite the heat, he was wearing a suit and tie.

"Well, well, well," Dr. Warsaw said, a thin sneer on his lips. "If it isn't the McDonald twins!"

Coke struggled to push open the door of the vapor cabinet, but Dr. Warsaw had obviously locked it securely shut when the lights were out. Pep let out a shriek.

"Go ahead and yell all you want, Miss Pepsi," Dr. Warsaw told her. "Nobody will hear you, but it's a great way to . . . let off a little steam."

He took a moment to laugh at his little joke.

"What are *you* doing here?" Coke demanded.

"Me?" said Dr. Warsaw. "I came here for two reasons. After our little altercation back at The Infinity Room, most of my large bones and internal organs were quite damaged, to say the least. The doctors told me I might never walk again. But they suggested I come here for my rehabilitation. The mineral waters have worked wonders to heal me. I'm almost a hundred percent now."

"So, what's the *other* reason you came here?" asked Pep.

"Oh, to kill you, of course," Dr. Warsaw said matter-of-factly. "The healing waters may have saved *my* life, but I'm sorry to say that they will have the opposite effect on yours."

"You're insane!"

"Let us out!"

"I never expected you two to make it this far," Dr. Warsaw said quietly as he paced around the twins. "I thought I had gotten rid of you back in Cleveland at the Rock and Roll Hall of Fame. I'll say one thing about you brats. You are quite resourceful."

Coke fumbled around desperately inside the vapor cabinet, trying to find a latch or switch that would open it up. He knew that some cars had such things in the trunk, in case people get trapped inside. No such luck this time.

"Let me tell you a little story," Dr. Warsaw said soothingly. "It's sort of a . . . bedtime story, you might say."

"We don't want to hear your stupid stories!" Coke spat. "Let us out of here and if you're lucky we won't press charges."

"Oh, you'll be able to relate to this story," Dr. Warsaw said. "It's the story of the boiling frog. You see, if you drop a frog into a pot of boiling water, it will frantically try to jump out to save its own life. That makes sense, right? But if you put that same frog in a pot of *cold* water and put a high flame under it, the frog won't notice that anything is wrong. It won't be frightened. And as the temperature slowly rises, degree by degree, the frog will just sit there and allow itself to slowly *boil to death*!"

"What's your point?" Pep shouted.

"Oh," Dr. Warsaw said, "you might say it's a metaphor for our inability to react to changes that occur gradually."

"You're crazy!" Coke shouted. "And that story is terrible!"

"Let us out of here!" shouted Pep.

"Oh, I'll let you out," Dr. Warsaw said, his mood darkening. "But first tell me something. Where's my

wife? Where's your aunt Judy? You must know where she is. I haven't heard from her in three days. What did you do to her?"

"We didn't do *anything* to her!" Coke said defiantly.

Dr. Warsaw went over to a control panel on the wall, about ten feet from the vapor cabinets.

"I think I'll just turn the heat up a little," he said. "Maybe that will help you remember. They say the healing vapors are also good for the memory."

He turned a dial, causing a spray of hot vapor to shoot up inside the cabinets. Sweat was starting to bead up on the twins' faces. A few salty drops fell into Coke's eyes. They stung.

"It's hot!" Pep yelled. "It's so hot!"

"*Now* are you ready to tell me what you did to my wife?" asked Dr. Warsaw.

"It wasn't our fault!" Pep yelled at him. "We were at Graceland—"

"No, Pep!" Coke shouted. "Don't tell him!"

"Shut up, Coke!" Pep said. "Aunt Judy was dressed up as an Elvis impersonator, and she pulled a gun on us, for no reason. I knocked the gun out of her hand with a Frisbee and she chased us. She found us in our RV, and she started waving lighted matches around like a crazy person. One of them set my brother's backpack on fire. But she didn't know that the backpack was full of fireworks. We jumped out just before the fireworks ignited, and the whole RV exploded. We never saw Aunt Judy again."

Silence. Coke and Pep looked at Dr. Warsaw, expecting him to lash out at them in anger. Instead, his shoulders heaved and he began to weep.

"So that's it," he blubbered. "Judy was the love of my life. We were going to be together forever. And now she's gone."

It was hard to feel sorry for him, and the twins didn't. Locked inside the steaming vapor cabinets, they just stared at the pathetic man.

After a few minutes of sobbing, Dr. Warsaw pulled himself together. Once again, he looked like the face of indescribable evil.

"I see," he said, nodding his head. "I get the picture. At The House on the Rock you kids destroyed my iJolt, which was my life's work. And you almost killed me in the process. Then you killed Archie Clone, my young apprentice, in Washington. And now, you tell me you killed my wife! What is wrong with you two? Do you think it's normal for children to go around killing people?"

"It was self-defense!" Pep shouted.

"You killed your own aunt!" Dr. Warsaw shouted back.

"She was trying to kill us!" Coke shouted.

"Why don't you drop the little charade?" said Dr. Warsaw wearily. "You've done enough. You're not innocent little kids."

"B-but . . ."

"I'm through playing childish games," Dr. Warsaw said, going back to the control panel. "Now it's time to finish you off once and for all."

"Noooooooooo!"

"The part of the brain that controls thirst and hunger is called the hypothalamus," Dr. Warsaw said as he fiddled with the knobs. "It also controls the body's core temperature. Normal body temperature is 98.6 degrees Fahrenheit. I think I'll just turn this up a little more."

"We don't want to hear your biology lesson!" Coke shouted as he struggled desperately to open the vapor cabinet.

"The body cools itself by sweating, and allowing that sweat to evaporate," Dr. Warsaw continued. "This requires enough fluid in the body to make sweat, air circulating across the skin, and low air humidity to allow that sweat to evaporate."

"Shut up!" Pep yelled.

"You're probably getting a little thirsty by now," Dr. Warsaw said, waving a water bottle in front of her face. "I bet you'd like a drink of this."

"Turn it down!" Coke said, his face bathed in sweat. "Turn the thing down!"

"Did you say turn it *up*?" asked Dr. Warsaw. "Sure! I'd be happy to turn it up."

"Down!" Coke yelled. "Turn it *down*!"

"When your body temperature gets to one hundred degrees, you have a fever," said Dr. Warsaw. "Your sweat gland activity increases. Blood flow to the skin increases. The hair on your arms and legs lies flat so the heat is not trapped close to your body."

"Help!" Pep screamed. "He's crazy! Somebody! Let us out of here!"

"Your body temperature keeps going up," Dr. Warsaw said. "If sweating isn't enough to cool the body and you don't replace the fluids, you become dehydrated. That can lead to heat exhaustion."

"Hellllllllp!"

"You're extremely thirsty now. Your skin is getting pale and clammy. You feel dizzy and weak. Your pulse is going up. Soon you'll start to feel a throbbing headache, nausea, and muscle cramps."

"I don't want to hear it!" Coke shouted. "Why do you psychos always have to explain how you're going to kill people?"

"Oh, that's part of the fun, Coke," Dr. Warsaw said.

"If your body temperature gets above 103 degrees, your hypothalamus becomes overwhelmed. Your body temperature regulation fails. Heat stroke sets in. You become confused and lethargic. You may have a seizure. I love seizures! Aren't seizures fun?"

"Turn it off!" Coke shouted. "I'll do anything you want. Just turn it off!"

But Dr. Warsaw ignored his pleas.

"The next step is hyperthermia," he said, excitement in his eyes. "Your proteins start to denature and break down. The electrical impulses in your nerves and muscles start to fire sporadically. If your temperature reaches 106 degrees, your brain is no longer able to perform the necessary functions to continue life. Vital organs shut down. You stop breathing, then your heart stops beating. And, well, I don't need to go into all the gory details, do I?"

"You already did!" Coke screamed.

"So I did," Dr. Warsaw agreed. *"Aha-ha-ha-ha-ha-ha!"*

His evil, cackling laugh echoed off the walls for a few moments until Pep said something that shut him up.

"How could Aunt Judy love you?" she screamed. "How could *anyone* love you?"

Quite suddenly, Dr. Warsaw stopped laughing and began to weep uncontrollably once again. He certainly was a man of many moods.

"I . . . can't do it," he said, leaning against the wall and burying his head in his arm.

The twins breathed a sigh of relief.

"Well, how about letting us go, then?" Pep asked.

"What's happening to me?" Dr. Warsaw moaned between sobs. "I used to be able to kill so easily, with no hesitation. No guilt. No remorse. And now look at me! I can't bring myself to kill a couple of spoiled brats like you two. What's wrong with me?"

"Maybe you're becoming sane," Pep suggested, trying to remain calm. "It's a *good* thing."

Dr. Warsaw came over to her vapor cabinet and slipped a key into the lock.

"I tried to do something good for the world," he sobbed. "The Genius Files was supposed to make the world a better place."

"We know," Pep said quietly. "We know."

"If you tell *anybody* I let you go, I'll kill you for sure," he warned Pep, staring into her eyes. "That includes your parents. Do you understand me?"

"Y-yes!" Pep stammered.

"We won't tell anybody," Coke said.

Dr. Warsaw opened both locks and stumbled out of the room sobbing, inconsolable. He was a broken man.

Coke and Pep pushed open the doors of their vapor cabinets. They were weak and a little wobbly, but they managed to stumble out of the room and downstairs to the front desk. The woman who had greeted them was still behind the counter.

"Did you see a weird-looking guy wearing a suit and tie?" Pep asked breathlessly.

"No, why? Is he okay?"

"No, he's crazy," Coke told her. "He must have snapped."

"Maybe he climbed out a window," Pep guessed.

They considered giving chase, but thought better of it. Dr. Warsaw was gone, hopefully forever.

Pep remembered that her mother's birthday would be in two days, and she dragged her brother into the little gift shop to look for a present. A package of soothing bath salts seemed like a good idea. She also bought a little refrigerator magnet in the shape of Arkansas. Pep had just finished paying when

their parents came in. Both of them were beaming.

"My Swedish massage was *fantastic*!" Dr. McDonald enthused. "I feel like I'm floating."

"I feel like I'm five years younger," said Mrs. McDonald. "Do you kids feel more relaxed now?"

"No!" they barked simultaneously. "Can we get out of here?"

Go to Google Maps (http://maps.google.com).

Click Get Directions.

In the A box, type Hot Springs AR.

In the B box, type Poteau OK.

Click Get Directions.

Chapter 9

THE JOY OF ARKANSAS

At this point, you might be getting a little bit angry because we're eight chapters into the book and Coke hasn't been shoved into a spinning clothes dryer yet.

Don't you hate that? You open a book and the author promises you in Chapter One that one of the characters is going to get shoved into a spinning clothes dryer. Then you read and read and read, and Coke still hasn't been shoved into a spinning clothes dryer. You want to read about some good spinning in a clothes dryer, and you're tired of waiting for it. You feel ripped off.

Again, dear reader, I ask for your continued patience. I said that Coke would be shoved into a spinning clothes dryer, and I promise you that before the end of the story, Coke will indeed be shoved into a spinning clothes dryer.

In fact, this book comes with a money-back guarantee. If, by the final chapter, Coke still hasn't been shoved into a spinning clothes dryer, you will receive a full refund. No questions asked.

For now, let's get back to the story. In the car after leaving the Quapaw spa, Coke and Pep did their best to put the strange confrontation with Dr. Warsaw out of their minds. It seemed as though the guy had finally lost his marbles, and thankfully was in no condition to do anyone harm. But with crazy people, you always have to stay on your guard.

There was something about being in the car that made the twins feel safer. The RV had felt like a rolling prison. But the little Ferrari was almost like a steel cocoon that would protect them from harm. They felt private and free.

After some debate about whether or not they should visit the Arkansas Alligator Farm in Hot Springs (Coke was the only one who really wanted to go), the McDonalds decided to "blow this pop stand" instead.

His mind and body refreshed, his pores fully opened, Dr. McDonald was so relaxed that he decided to turn off the GPS. He put the car in drive, and just drove. The compass said they were heading WEST, and that was good enough for him. Soon the family found themselves on Albert Pike Road, also known as U.S. Route 270.

There are more than 53,000 square miles in Arkansas, and there are a lot of interesting places worth seeing. Inside the Ferrari, a great debate commenced to determine which sites were worth stopping at, and which ones should be bypassed.

Dr. McDonald cast his vote for a side trip to Bentonville, where Sam Walton opened up the first Walmart in 1962.

"There's a museum there now," Mrs. McDonald said, reading from her guidebook.

"Gee, what a shock," Coke said with his usual eye roll.

He voted to visit the town of Eureka Springs, where the Museum of Fake Frogs is located. According to the guidebook, the old man who runs it has been accumulating frog collectibles for fifty years, and now he's up to six thousand frog-themed items.

Coke insisted that anything to do with frogs was cool, but if he couldn't go there, he would instead be willing to see (and use) one of the world's only double-decker outhouses, which is in Dover, Arkansas.

Don't believe me? Go ahead and look it up. That's why they invented Google.

Pep was always fascinated by morbid curiosities such as the Donner Party, settlers who resorted to cannibalism to survive the winter of 1846 in the Sierra Nevada. So when she heard about the Boggy Creek Monster in Fouke, Arkansas, she was intrigued.

The monster, sort of a southern version of Bigfoot, is supposed to be seven feet tall and hairy all over. It has been known to kill and eat chickens, cattle, dogs, and livestock, if not small children.

It was highly unlikely that they would actually catch a glimpse of the Boggy Creek Monster, so Pep said her second choice was to visit Crater of Diamonds State Park, in Murfreesboro, Arkansas. It's the only diamond-producing site in the world that's open to the public. In fact, in 2007, a thirteen-year-old girl found a 2.9-carat diamond there.

Mrs. McDonald, as always, was on the lookout for new material she could use in *Amazing but True*. But

it was difficult to choose from the wealth of oddball tourist attractions in Arkansas.

"Maybe we should go to Alma," she suggested. "It's the Spinach Capital of the World."

"No more capitals!"

"We could go to Stuttgart and see the World's Championship Duck Calling Contest," said Mrs. McDonald.

There was just too much to see in Arkansas. Obviously, they couldn't do it all. There are only twenty-four hours in a day, as they say, and you've got to sleep sometime.

The discussion continued as the McDonalds drove past Lake Hamilton and through the little towns of Royal, Joplin, and Hurricane Grove. The Caddo Mountains were in the distance now, and soon they were deep within Ouachita National Forest and Queen Wilhelmina State Park, drinking in the spectacular scenery.

Sometimes we spend so much time and energy thinking about where we want to go that we don't notice where we happen to be.

The McDonald family was still discussing which sites to visit in Arkansas when a sign appeared at the side of the road. . . .

Chapter 10

TOP OF THE WORLD

So much for Arkansas. They crossed the Oklahoma state line.

Spontaneously—and inevitably—the entire McDonald family burst into the song "Oklahoma!" from the 1955 Rogers and Hammerstein musical of the same name. I would print the lyrics for you here, but we would have to pay a lot of money for the rights, so forget that idea. YouTube it, and you can hear the whole song for free.

"*Woo-hoo!*" Coke shouted when the family couldn't remember the words to the second verse. "We're in the Sooner State, baby! Hey, ya know why Oklahoma is called the Sooner State?"

"Nobody cares!" Pep shouted.

"I'll bet you guys can't name four things that were invented in Oklahoma," Coke said.

"Here we go," grumbled Pep.

"Genetically engineered soybeans?" guessed Dr. McDonald.

"No, it was the shopping cart, the aerosol can, the parking meter, and the automated twist tie machine!" Coke proclaimed proudly. He had learned this while Googling "American inventions."

"Is that so?" said his father.

After all these years, he never ceased to be impressed by the amount of seemingly worthless information his son could hold in his head. It was as though Coke's brain was a hard drive with unlimited gigabyte storage, and nothing ever got deleted.

Outside, one of the prettiest parts of Oklahoma was passing by. They don't call it the Talimena Scenic Drive for nothing. The road winds fifty-four spectacular miles along the mountaintops, with lush green forests, meadows full of wildflowers, and a smoky blue haze in the distance. The McDonalds were craning their necks in all directions to take in the scenery.

"Look! A bear!" Pep shouted suddenly.

"Where?"

"Over there!"

And so it was. A black bear on the right side of the road gamboled off into the woods.

It was past three o'clock now, which meant it was time to start thinking about a place to stop for the night. When they had the RV, they were able to just pull over into any parking lot, if necessary, to sleep. Ferraris are fine cars, but you'll never hear people say they want to sleep in one. Certainly not a family of four. And not with bears around.

Mrs. McDonald dropped her Arkansas guidebook into the trash bag and pulled out *Oklahoma Off the Beaten Path*. She discovered that Poteau, an old coal-mining town, was only a half hour away. The guidebook said there were three hotels there, so Mrs. McDonald called on her cell phone and made a reservation at the Holiday Inn Express. She punched the address into the GPS and leafed through her guidebook to find out if there was anything in the area worth seeing.

"Hey, you won't believe this!" she blurted out. "The world's highest hill is in Poteau. It's called Cavanal Hill."

"No kidding?" said Dr. McDonald.

"Never heard of it," said Coke.

"I thought Mount Everest was the highest," said Pep.

Intrigued, the family agreed to stop by Cavanal Hill before checking into the hotel for the night. A few miles west and slightly north of town, it wasn't hard to find.

"Wait a minute," Coke said as he got out of the car. "This mountain doesn't look all that high. How can they say it's the highest one in the world?"

"It's not a mountain," a tall guy with a fancy bike in the parking lot told him. "It's a *hill*."

"What's the difference?" Pep asked.

"A mountain has to be at least two thousand feet high," the guy explained. "Anything less than that is a hill."

"And how high is this hill?" asked Dr. McDonald.

"One thousand, nine hundred and ninety-nine feet," the guy replied.

"You mean to say that if Cavanal Hill was just one foot higher it would be the world's shortest mountain?" asked Mrs. McDonald. "But because of some dumb rule it's the world's highest hill?"

"You got it," said the guy with the bike.

"That's bogus!" shouted Coke. "This place is a rip-off!"

"It can't be a rip-off," Pep told him. "It doesn't cost anything."

"I don't care," Coke said. "It's still a rip-off. It's false advertising."

"There's no ad either!" Pep said.

"I'll tell you what it is," Mrs. McDonald said, reaching for her notepad. "It's perfect for *Amazing but True.* My readers will love this."

While Cavanal is no Everest, the tree-covered hill draws hikers, bikers, and runners from all over who want to climb it. In fact, the hike to the top is called "the Cavanal Killer." The nickname alone made Coke and Pep want to reach the summit.

"You kids go on ahead," said Dr. McDonald. "It still looks pretty high to me. Mom and I will wait down here with the other *old* fogies."

Coke and Pep looked at each other. The same memory flashed through both of their minds—the Singing Sand Dunes in Nevada, where they had been just a few weeks earlier. Their parents had waited in the parking lot while they hiked up the mountain of sand. When they reached the top, they were confronted by a nut in a bowler hat who threw them into a pit and left them there to die. If Coke hadn't hit the guy in the back of the head with a jar full of sand, they would probably still be up there today.

Or their skeletons would be, anyway.

Of course, that seemed like ages ago. Nobody was

chasing them anymore. Mrs. Higgins was working at the Bauxite Museum. Dr. Warsaw had had some sort of a mental meltdown back in Hot Springs. The last time they saw the bowler dudes, it was at Coca-Cola World in Atlanta. There was probably nothing to worry about. Mya and Bones had told them as much. They said the coast was clear.

Coke and Pep started climbing the mountain—I mean, the *hill*. It was a challenging hike, but hardly qualified as a *killer*. It was a cloudless day, and when they reached the top, they were treated to a spectacular panoramic view of the Poteau River valley. Mount Magazine, in Arkansas, was visible in the distance. No other people were around.

"It's so calm and peaceful up here," Coke said, closing his eyes and taking in a deep breath of fresh air.

"I don't know," Pep replied. "I have the feeling that somebody's following us."

"You and your feelings."

Coke strolled over to read the concrete sign at the top of Cavanal Hill. Pep followed him but suddenly stopped in her tracks.

"What's that noise?" she asked.

"What noise? I don't hear any noise."

They looked up, and sure enough, high overhead, they could see a dot in the sky.

"I'll bet it's a drone!" Pep said. "They use them to track down terrorists! And kill them!"

"It's not a drone," Coke said with a snort. "Now you're being ridiculous."

He was right. It wasn't a drone. It was a plane—one of those small, two-seater propeller planes. It appeared to be circling.

"They probably give aerial tours," Coke added, craning his neck to follow the path of the plane.

"What if it's spying on us?" Pep asked.

"You're paranoid," her brother replied.

Coke was about to look away when two objects appeared to tumble out of the plane. From such a distance, it was impossible to tell what they were.

But then, seconds later, two brightly colored parachutes opened.

Whatever the falling objects were, they were falling directly over Coke and Pep. The twins hesitated for a moment, transfixed by the sight of the parachutes floating down so gracefully.

Soon it was clear that the objects hanging from the parachutes were people. And it didn't take much longer for the twins to figure out who the people were.

"Bowler dudes at twelve o'clock!" Coke shouted, pointing at them. "Run for it, Pep!"

The twins took off, running east on a concrete path that led away from the Cavanal Hill sign.

"I *told* you somebody was following us!" Pep shouted breathlessly.

Coke turned around for an instant to see the parachuting bowler dudes right behind them and descending rapidly. They were only about thirty feet overhead now. Their chutes were the kind that can be steered, and the dudes were steering them directly toward the twins.

"Just *run*!" Coke shouted at his sister. "Head for the trees!"

The parachuting bowler dudes were closing fast, and the twins could hear them as they ran for their lives.

"Ha-ha-ha-ha-ha-ha!" one of the bowler dudes cackled. "We've got you now!"

Coke felt like his heart was about to burst in his chest as he ran for the trees. Just a few more yards. He knew that if he and Pep could just make it into the woods, the parachutes would—

Craaaaaaackkkkk.

It was the sound of a tree branch breaking.

"Ooooooof!"

"Owwwww!"

It was the sound of two bowler dudes moaning.

The twins, exhausted, couldn't help but stop and turn around. Looking up into the tree behind them, they could see the mustachioed bowler dude with his arms and legs wrapped around a tree trunk, and hanging on for dear life. The clean-shaven bowler dude was dangling helplessly from his parachute cord, which was tangled in the branches above.

"You *idiot*!" said the mustachioed bowler dude, hanging from the tree. "I told you to go left!"

"I *went* left!" complained his clean-shaven brother. "You don't even know your left from your right, you moron!"

"*You're* a moron!"

"No, *you're* a moron!"

"You're *both* morons!" Coke said, pointing at them and laughing. "Have fun getting down from there. Come on, Pep."

The twins were about to run away when the mustachioed bowler dude called out to them.

"Wait!" he shouted. "Help us down, will ya?"

"Yeah, we could die up here," his brother said.

"Are you *kidding* me?" Pep shouted up at them. You expect us to help you after all you've done to us? You're crazy!"

"Look, we don't have any weapons," said the clean-shaven bowler dude. "We're completely defenseless."

"Then why do you keep following us?" Pep asked. "What did we ever do to *you*?"

"We didn't come here to hurt you," said the mustachioed bowler dude. "We came here to deliver a message."

"What message?" Coke said skeptically.

"The message is that it's all over," said the clean-shaven bowler dude. "You don't need to fear us, or anybody, anymore. You can enjoy the rest of your vacation. We're sorry for what we did to you, and it won't happen again. Now will you help us down, please?"

The twins looked at the bowler dudes. The sincerity on their faces appeared to be so genuine, they just *had* to be faking it.

"We don't believe a word of that," Pep said. "You lied to us before."

"That's right," Coke said, pointing an accusing finger. "Back in Maryland, you told us you had given up hurting kids to devote yourselves to jousting. And then, a few days later, you tried to hurt us when we got to Atlanta."

"We were employed by Dr. Warsaw at that time," said the mustachioed bowler dude. "It was our *job* to hurt you. But we no longer work for him."

"Oh, I get it. You were only following orders," Coke said disdainfully. "That's what the Nazis said."

"You've got to believe us," said the mustachioed bowler dude. "*Please* help us down. I'm afraid I'm going to fall and crack my head on the ground."

"Why should we believe you *now*?" Pep asked.

"Look," the clean-shaven bowler dude told her, "it doesn't matter if you believe us or not. But consider the facts. Dr. Warsaw has suffered some sort of a mental breakdown. He's no longer paying us, and as you know, we work for the people who pay us. If nobody pays us to hurt you, we won't hurt you. It's simple economics."

The bowler dude with his arms and legs wrapped around the tree had a look of panic on his face. His grip was starting to slip.

Coke would have been willing to let the guy fall, and have a good laugh when he hit the ground. Pep, however, was unable to watch another human being in such distress and do nothing. Something about feelings.

"Come on," she said to her brother. "If they die out here, it will be our fault. As it is, I feel terrible about what happened to Archie Clone and Evil Elvis."

The twins grabbed onto a low branch and pulled themselves up the tree. Carefully, they helped the mustachioed bowler dude down. Meanwhile, his brother managed to climb up his parachute cord, unfasten his harness, and shimmy down the tree.

"The Genius Files program is dead," he said when he reached the ground. "You're free. You can live your lives, or be paranoid for the rest of your lives if you want to. It's your choice. That's all we came here to say."

The twins looked them up and down. Neither of the bowler dudes appeared to have a blowgun or any other weapon on him.

"You won't bother us anymore?" Pep asked.

"Cross my heart and hope to die," said the

mustachioed bowler dude. "We won't follow you. We won't chase you. All we ask is that you keep quiet so we can start new lives for ourselves without any fear of prosecution. Okay?"

"Okay."

Coke and Pep took a few steps backward, watching the bowler dudes the whole time to see if they were going to try something. The dudes put their hands in the air, as if to say they were not going to throw anything, and they were not going to shoot anything.

"Go, Pep!" Coke shouted, and they just about broke the land speed record running down Cavanal Hill.

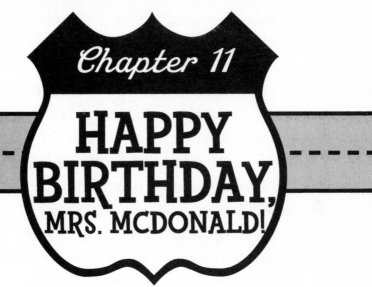

Chapter 11

HAPPY BIRTHDAY, MRS. MCDONALD!

So the coast was truly clear. The bowler dudes weren't going to hurt them. Mrs. Higgins wasn't going to hurt them. Dr. Warsaw wasn't going to hurt them.

"This is the best vacation I ever had," Coke told his parents enthusiastically. "I just wanted to let you guys know that I'm having a wonderful time."

"Me too," Pep added brightly. "Driving cross-country is so much more of an enriching experience than going to some dumb theme park."

In the front seat, the parents looked at each other

suspiciously. Something had to be up. Neither of them could remember the last time the twins were so cheery and cooperative.

After a fantastic dinner at Western Sizzlin in Poteau, the McDonalds pulled into the parking lot at the Holiday Inn Express.

"How is this place any different from a *regular* Holiday Inn?" Pep asked as her parents checked in at the front desk.

"Maybe you sleep faster here," Coke cracked.

When they got to their room, Pep was careful to hide the birthday present she had gotten for her mother, a box of soothing bath salts she had picked up back in Hot Springs, Arkansas. Coke, who remembered just about every *other* thing he had ever experienced, never remembered anybody's birthday. Pep knew her present would have to be from the two of them.

"Only a few more hours until the big day, Bridge," said Dr. McDonald as he unpacked his suitcase. "Tomorrow, you're in charge. We do whatever *you* want to do. You can boss us around all you want."

"Really?"

"Sure," said Dr. McDonald. "Do you want to go out to a fancy restaurant for dinner? Fine. You want to sit around the hotel pool all day? That's okay too. Whatever your heart desires, honey."

Mrs. McDonald thought it over. The money she made from *Amazing but True* was paying for the trip, and she pretty much decided what they would do *every* day. But she was always conscious of the rest of the family's boredom level, and tried not to drag them to places that wouldn't interest them.

But it was her birthday. All bets were off. This was going to be *her* day. She decided to make the most of it.

"I can do anything I want?" she asked.

"*Anything,*" said Dr. McDonald.

"Okay," Mrs. McDonald said. "Everybody needs to be ready to get on the road at seven o'clock."

"Where are we going, Mom?" Pep asked.

"You'll see."

While the others slept, Mrs. McDonald spent the next two hours with a guidebook, a map of Oklahoma, and her laptop computer. In the morning, after the presents, singing "Happy Birthday," and a quick continental breakfast, they piled into the car and drove a very fast eighty miles north to Tahlequah, Oklahoma.

Usually, Mrs. McDonald was telling her husband to slow down and observe all the speed limit signs. Not today.

"Faster, Ben!" Mrs. McDonald kept urging. "You drive like a glacier!"

"I'm doing seventy miles an hour," Dr. McDonald complained. "If I go any faster, we're gonna get pulled over."

"Why did you buy a Ferrari if you didn't want to drive fast?" she replied.

"What's your rush?" asked Dr. McDonald. "We've got all day."

"Floor it, Dad!" Coke hollered from the backseat.

It only took an hour and a half to reach Tahlequah, in the foothills of the Ozark Mountains. Just outside town, Mrs. McDonald directed them to a little ranch house, which appeared to be abandoned. Dr. McDonald parked across the road and they walked around back, where there was a metal shed.

"This place is creepy," Pep said.

On the ground to the left of the shed was a large tombstone. It looked like it had once been standing up, but somebody knocked it over. This is what it said on the tombstone. . . .

Mister ED

"Who's Mister Ed?" Coke asked.

"You never heard of Mister Ed?" his mother replied.

When the twins shook their heads no, both parents spontaneously broke into a silly song that began with the words "A horse is a horse, of course, of course...."

Once again, I wish I could give you all the lyrics, but financial considerations as well as personal laziness prevent that from happening. Instead, go to YouTube and search for "Mister Ed theme song."

Go ahead, we'll wait for you here.

"*Mister Ed* was my favorite show when I was a kid," said Dr. McDonald.

"They made a TV show about a talking horse?" Coke asked.

"Well, he only talked to Wilbur, his owner," explained Dr. McDonald.

"Sometimes he talked on the phone too," Mrs. McDonald added. "I heard they made him talk by putting a nylon thread in his mouth and pulling on it."

The tombstone had an etching of Mister Ed poking his head through a barn door. Mrs. McDonald took some photos and explained that Mister Ed's original name was Bamboo Harvester.

"So, there's a horse buried under here?" Coke asked.

"Yes, but nobody is sure it's Mister Ed," Mrs. McDonald told them. "Some people say he died in 1970 in California. Others say he died here in Oklahoma, in 1979."

"With all due respect, Mom," Pep said, "a TV show about a talking horse sounds really dumb to me."

"You're lucky you never saw *My Mother the Car*," said Dr. McDonald.

"And they say *today's* TV shows are lame," Coke said, shaking his head.

"Okay, let's go, gang," Mrs. McDonald announced.

"That's it?" asked Coke. "I wanted to look around."

"Sorry," his mother said. "It's my birthday and what I say goes."

In no time they were pushing the speed limit on Route 62 West, heading for downtown Muskogee. They made it in half an hour. Dr. McDonald found a parking spot a block from Three Rivers Museum. But they didn't go inside the museum. Mrs. McDonald walked over to a bronze statue of a little girl out front.

"Behold!" she said with a sweep of her arm. "The site of the first Girl Scout cookie sale!"

The statue was of a Girl Scout, with her sash covered in merit badges, and three fingers raised. There were four boxes of Girl Scout cookies at her feet. Mrs. McDonald pulled out her camera to shoot photos for *Amazing but True*. A few people ducked out of the way to avoid getting into the shot.

"Oh man!" Coke whined. "We drove all the way over here to see *this*?"

"Today is *Mom's* day," his father whispered, pulling him to the side. "So we're going to do whatever Mom wants to do. No complaining, understand?"

Mrs. McDonald explained that just five years after Juliette Gordon Low started Girl Scouting in 1912, the first Girl Scout cookies were sold in Muskogee, Oklahoma. The Mistletoe Troop baked the cookies themselves, and the profits were used to send gifts to American soldiers fighting in World War I.

The family had only been looking at the statue for a few minutes when Mrs. McDonald abruptly announced it was time to "blow this pop stand."

Following her, the family hopped in the car and drove sixty-eight miles, mainly on I-40 West, to the town of Okemah. It took about an hour. A mile off the exit, Mrs. McDonald directed them to Highland Cemetery. After a few minutes of searching, she found what she was looking for.

"Behold!" she said grandly.

"What is this?"

It was an ordinary-looking tombstone of a woman named Barbara Sue Manire. But right next to it, sticking out of the granite, was something you wouldn't expect to see in a cemetery—a parking meter.

On the meter were the words: 64 YEAR TIME LIMIT. TIME EXPIRED.

BARBARA SUE MANIRE
APR. 29, 1941
APR. 29, 2005
OUR MOM...
HER HUMOR LIVES ON

"She died on her sixty-fourth birthday," Mrs. McDonald said solemnly. "Her time ran out."

"The parking meter was invented right here in Oklahoma, y'know," Coke said. "A guy named Carl Magee patented it in Oklahoma City, in 1935."

"Only a true dork would know that," Pep said.

"Don't call your brother a dork," her father warned.

"Okay, let's get out of here," Mrs. McDonald said, putting away her camera.

"Can we go someplace for lunch now?" Coke asked when they were back in the car. "I'm starved."

"Have a sandwich," she said, flipping two into the backseat. "No time for stops today. Hit the gas, Ben!"

Heading west, it took less than an hour to reach the famous Route 66. When they saw the sign, Dr. and

Mrs. McDonald broke into song again, warbling the classic "(Get Your Kicks on) Route 66."

YouTube it. Dozens of people have recorded this song. I recommend the Nat King Cole version.

Before the interstate highway system was built, Route 66 was the longest road in America, and was called "the Mother Road." Just two lanes, it stretched 2,500 miles, all the way from Chicago to Los Angeles.

Mrs. McDonald directed them along Route 66 to what looked like an old gas station in the tiny town of Warwick. It *was* a gas station a long time ago. Today, it's the Seaba Station Motorcycle Museum.

"Choppers are cool!" Coke said as he rushed inside.

The museum has more than sixty vintage motorcycles dating back to 1908, as well as racing uniforms,

magazines, posters, parts, tools, toys, signs, and an Evel Knievel pinball machine. But almost as soon as they walked in the door, Mrs. McDonald was hurrying the family out again.

"Let's go! Let's go!" she shouted. "You've seen one motorcycle, you've seen 'em all."

By this time, Coke and Pep had almost completely forgotten that for much of this trip, a team of psychos had been trying to kill them.

Only nineteen miles west of the motorcycle museum, they came to *another* old gas station along Route 66, in the picturesque town of Arcadia. This

one still pumps gas, but it is also a convenience store and restaurant called Pops. Standing in front of it is "Bubbles"—the world's largest pop bottle.

"It is . . . *huge!*" Mrs. McDonald said as she reached for her camera.

The bottle is sixty-six feet tall. (That is, if you include the giant straw sticking out the top.) If they had been there at night, the McDonalds would have seen it glowing.

Pops was jammed with customers, with a forty-five-minute wait to get a table. Mrs. McDonald was in a rush, and so she led the family to the convenience store, where nearly five hundred varieties of pop were for sale. She bought a bottle of something called Moxie. The twins bought a Coke and a Pepsi, of course.

"Are you having a nice birthday, Bridge?" Dr. McDonald asked when they were back in the car.

"This is my dream day," she replied, thanking him with a smooch. "I love you so much for letting me do this."

"I love you too."

"Ugh, gross!" Pep yelled.

"Will you two knock it off before I get sick?" Coke shouted from the backseat. "We don't need to see that."

It was afternoon by this time, and Mrs. McDonald still had a lot she wanted to see in Oklahoma. From Arcadia, it was just half an hour to Oklahoma City, the capital and the largest city in the state. It is also—from the standpoint of *Amazing but True* fans—the greatest city in America. In this one town, the McDonalds

were able to visit the American Banjo Museum, the National Softball Hall of Fame, the National Cowboy Museum, and the Museum of Osteology.

If you don't know what *osteology* means, it is the study of bones. They have over three hundred skeletons and four hundred skulls! Pep claimed to be totally grossed out by it all, but that didn't stop her from buying a glow-in-the-dark black scorpion acrylic bottle opener in the gift shop. She also got a refrigerator magnet in the shape of Oklahoma. Pep thought it might be fun to start a collection of refrigerator magnets.

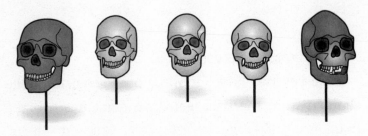

Visiting the museums in Oklahoma City had been strictly a hit-and-run operation. It was in and out of each one in half an hour, tops.

"We barely saw any of those places," Coke complained.

"At least we can say we were there," his mother replied. "That's the important thing."

It was almost four o'clock. Any *normal* tourist

would have had enough sightseeing for one day, but Mrs. McDonald wasn't finished yet. As the car headed south along I-35, she directed the family to the town of Pauls Valley, where they stopped off at the Toy and Action Figure Museum.

Who knew that in the middle of Oklahoma there would be a building that was stuffed to the rafters with thirteen thousand action figures? The place might as well be called Nerd Heaven. If you go, be sure to check out the Bat Cave.

Coke could have spent hours looking at all the stuff at the Toy and Action Figure Museum, but it closed at five o'clock and the family was hustled out the door.

"So, where are we going for dinner?" Pep asked, assuming the day's activities were finally over.

But they weren't. Mrs. McDonald had planned the day down to the minute, and she knew that the Ardmore Public Library in Ardmore, Oklahoma, was open until eight o'clock. And the library just happened to be the home of the Eliza Cruce Hall Doll Museum. The McDonalds jumped back on I-35 South and raced thirty-four miles so they could see three hundred rare and antique dolls made out of porcelain, bisque, leather, wood, and even wax. The highlight of the collection is some carved wooden French dolls that were once owned by Marie Antoinette.

Pep wanted to examine each one. But by this time, the boys were feeling like their stomachs were starting to devour themselves.

"We're starving, Mom!" Coke begged. "Can't we go eat now?"

"Yeah," agreed his father. "Haven't we done enough for one day, Bridge?"

"Almost," she replied. "We need to get on Route 70 East. Let's go!"

Reluctantly, the rest of the family got back in the car and dragged themselves another hour to the quiet city of Durant.

"What lame museum do they have here?" Coke asked. He thought he might faint if he didn't get something to eat soon.

"This is the last place we're going to visit today," Mrs. McDonald said. "I promise!"

"What could possibly be open at this hour?" Coke asked.

"You'll see."

Dr. McDonald did as he was told, turning on to Evergreen Street and sliding into a parking spot at the corner of Third Street. There was some sort of a monument in front of the city hall building there.

"What is it?" Pep asked.

"Behold!" Mrs. McDonald proclaimed. "It's the

world's largest peanut!"

And so it was.

Well, to be fair, the people of Ashburn, Georgia, also claim to have the world's largest peanut. But there was no denying that the peanut monument in front of the Durant City Hall was quite large, and deserved some recognition.

It had been some day. The McDonalds had driven over 430 miles across Oklahoma. They had visited twelve sites. Mrs. McDonald had gathered a tremendous amount of material for *Amazing but True*.

"I'm beat!" Dr. McDonald said as he slid into the booth at a Mexican restaurant called Taco Casa.

"This has been the most wonderful birthday I can remember," Mrs. McDonald said, "even though there were a few places in Oklahoma we didn't get to."

"What could we possibly have missed, Mom?" Coke asked.

"Well," she said, "Geronimo's grave is in Fort Sill. We didn't make it there. The Wrestling Hall of Fame is in Stillwater. Beaver, Oklahoma, is the Cow Chip Throwing Capital of the World. And there's a man in Nowata who has fourteen hundred bowling balls in his backyard."

She could have gone on and on.

The Comfort Inn was relatively inexpensive, so instead of jamming the whole family into one small room, the parents had decided to splurge and put the twins in a room of their own. Coke and Pep were worn out after the long day, and didn't even bother to turn on the TV. They just brushed their teeth, put on their pajamas, turned off the light, and went to bed.

As soon as Coke's head hit the pillow, the phone next to his bed rang. He picked it up, assuming his parents were calling to say good night.

"Look under your pillow," said the voice at the other end of the line. It was a male voice, but it sounded

slightly robotic, as if it was computer generated.

"Who *is* this?" Coke asked.

"Look under your pillow," repeated the voice.

And then the line went dead.

Coke flipped the light on at his bedside.

"What's the matter?" Pep asked from the other bed. "Who was that?"

"I don't know," Coke replied as he reached under his pillow.

There was an envelope. He tore it open and this was written on a bright yellow piece of paper:

IWI LLME ETY OUIN LLANO ESTA CADO

"Oh no," Coke said.

He showed his sister the paper.

"Do you think it's . . ."

"Yeah," Pep replied. "It's a cipher."

Chapter 12

THE FIRST CIPHER

Coke and Pep stared at the message written on the slip of paper. . . .

IWI LLME ETY OUIN LLANO ESTA CADO

A secret code, as you may remember, disguises words or phrases. A cipher disguises individual letters. For centuries, people have been using these methods to send information without letting other people—their enemies—see it.

It doesn't even have to be a secret message. Any symbol or signal can represent something else. For instance, if you wanted to convey the idea of a four-legged furry creature that goes "meow," you would write the letters *C-A-T.* Anybody who knows that those letters represent a real cat—that is, anybody who knows how to read—will understand the message. That person cracked the code!

Of course, it's not usually that easy. Often, one letter is replaced with a different letter or a symbol to hide the meaning of the message. Sometimes the letters are simply rearranged.

Governments, companies, and spies and other people have come up with incredibly ingenious ways to keep their information secret. Like this one: Shave the head of your messenger and tattoo your message on his scalp. Then allow enough time for some of his hair to grow back. Then, the only way to decipher the message is to shave his head!

Coke and Pep never got their heads shaved. But ever since they left California, they had been receiving a new cipher every few days. At first, the ciphers were coming from Dr. Warsaw himself. After his "accident" at The House on the Rock, they were sent by his young madman-in-training Archie Clone. After the helicopter crash in Washington at the National Museum of American History, Evil Elvis/Aunt Judy was sending the twins ciphers.

But who sent this one? Dr. Warsaw had a nervous breakdown back in Hot Springs. He probably was in no condition to be messing with their heads. Archie Clone and Aunt Judy were no longer alive. The bowler dudes were incompetent idiots. Who could be sending them secret messages *now*? Mrs. Higgins? Somebody else?

And what could *IWI LLME ETY OUIN LLANO ESTA CADO* possibly mean?

Unlike her brother, Pep wasn't very good at absorbing and remembering vast quantities of information. She didn't have a photographic memory. But she was excellent at analyzing information, and in fact it was a hobby of hers. She had an uncanny ability to take a series of seemingly random letters, numbers, or symbols and juggle them around to reveal their secret meaning.

"I'm stumped," Coke said after looking at the cipher for a grand total of ten seconds. The boy had lots of good qualities, but a sustained attention span was not one of them. His sister, however, had already figured it out.

"Oh, come on. It's easy!" Pep told him. "They haven't even transposed any of the letters. All you have to do is group them differently. Watch."

She picked up the pen from the night table and began to write directly below the message. Instead of writing *IWI*, she wrote *I WILL*. Instead of writing *LLME ETY*, she wrote *MEET*.

"I will meet you!" Coke shouted, as if he was deciphering the message himself.

"Right," Pep agreed as she continued regrouping the letters. "*I WILL MEET YOU IN . . . LLANO ESTACADO.* Or Llano Esta Cado. What does 'Llano' mean? Or 'Esta Cado'? It looks Spanish."

"Llano Estacado is the part of the southwestern United States that encompasses eastern New Mexico and northwestern Texas," Coke said matter-of-factly.

"I think I should call you 'Google' from now on," Pep replied.

"But how does that help us?" Coke asked. "What are we supposed to do—meet somebody *somewhere* in Texas or New Mexico? Gee, that's a big help. Texas is more than 268,000 square miles. And when are we supposed to meet this mysterious person?"

"This doesn't help us at all," Pep said. "He's just teasing us. Or *she* is."

> Go to Google Maps (http://maps.google.com).
>
> Click Get Directions.
>
> In the A box, type Durant OK.
>
> In the B box, type Denison TX.
>
> Click Get Directions.

123

Chapter 13

WELCOME TO TEXAS

Coke and Pep had been sure their troubles were over. But that was yesterday. It felt like a dark cloud was gathering up ahead. If the coast was clear, why would anyone be sending them a mysterious message?

"I have a bad feeling about this," Pep said. And her feelings were pretty much on the mark.

Maybe it was just a meaningless, random message, Coke tried to convince himself as he struggled to go to sleep. Maybe it was meant for somebody else.

He tried desperately to remember the voice on the phone that told him to look under his pillow. He tried to connect it with someone he had met in his life. But there was nobody. It was a familiar voice, but not one that he had heard before.

The twins awoke to the sound of *USA Today* being slipped under their hotel room door. It was July 15th. The usual wars, murders, and natural disasters were going on in the world. But when they looked out the window, all appeared calm in southern Oklahoma.

Coke and Pep went downstairs to have breakfast with their parents, and then it was back on the road. Dr. McDonald merged onto Route 69 heading south.

The first argument of the day had already begun. Mrs. McDonald said they needed to stop at a laundromat sometime during the day, because they didn't have a lot of clothing after the RV exploded in Memphis. Dr. McDonald said he didn't want to waste time doing laundry, insisting there was no reason why they couldn't wear the same clothes for two days. Mrs. McDonald, of course, found that idea repulsive.

The argument didn't last long, because just a few minutes after they were on the road, they crossed a bridge over a river and this sign came into view on the left side of the highway. . . .

"*Woo hoo!*" Coke shouted at the top of his lungs, "The Lone Star State! Did you know that the Texas state mascot is the armadillo?"

"I actually *did* know that," said Pep. "But did *you* know that armadillos always have four babies?"

Coke was taken aback. He couldn't think of the last time his sister knew something that he didn't. He searched his memory bank. Never in his life had he heard anything about the number of babies armadillos had.

"You just made that up," he said.

"I did not," Pep told him. "I learned that when we went on a field trip to the natural history museum."

"Well, nobody cares how many babies armadillos have," Coke insisted.

"Armadillos care."

Mrs. McDonald dropped her Arkansas guidebook into the trash and pulled *Amazing Texas Monuments and Museums* out of her purse.

"They say everything is bigger in Texas, you know," she told the rest of the family. "The whole state stretches almost eight *hundred* miles each way."

"I read somewhere that the world's largest parking lot is at the Dallas/Fort Worth airport," Dr. McDonald said. "That airport is larger than the whole island of Manhattan."

"That's quite a claim to fame," remarked Coke. "They have the world's largest parking lot!"

"It says here that you could fit two hundred and twenty Rhode Islands into Texas," said Mrs. McDonald.

"They're always comparing the big states to Rhode Island," Pep said, rolling her eyes. "Why don't they leave poor little Rhode Island alone?"

Coke turned around to see if any cars might be following them. The road was nearly empty. It would take a while to get through Texas, and both twins settled in for a long drive. But just moments past the state line, Dr. McDonald suddenly pulled off the road after seeing a sign for the town of Denison. It was uncharacteristic for him. In general, he didn't do

things spontaneously.

"What's the matter, Ben?" asked Mrs. McDonald. "Are you okay?"

"Denison, Denison," Dr. McDonald repeated. "It rings a bell. I can't remember why."

He maneuvered the Ferrari off the ramp. As soon as he saw a sign that said EISENHOWER PARKWAY, he remembered.

"Of course!" he said. "Eisenhower *lived* here!"

Mrs. McDonald pulled out her laptop and quickly confirmed that the thirty-fourth president of the United States was born in Denison, Texas. He only lived in the town for the first two years of his life, but there's a monument dedicated to him.

She directed Dr. McDonald to take the exit for Loy Lake, and soon they found themselves on Loy Lake Road, at the entrance to Loy Lake Park. And there it was—a sixteen-foot cement head in the shape of Dwight David Eisenhower. The statue had a blank expression on its face.

"That is one gigantic head," Coke said, stating the obvious. "It may be the biggest head I've ever seen."

"What did Eisenhower do, Dad?" Pep asked.

"Oh, nothing important," replied Dr. McDonald. "He just organized the D-day invasion in World War Two. He liberated Europe from the Nazis. Defeated

Hitler. Won the war. Nothing to write home about."

"If not for President Eisenhower," said Mrs. McDonald, "we'd all be speaking German today."

"Isn't that what you said about bauxite?" asked Pep.

"Ich spreche Deutsch jetzt!" said Coke.

Back in the car and on the road, the twins were curious about what they were going to do—besides laundry, of course—in the great state of Texas.

"I really want to go to Paris," Mrs. McDonald said.

"That's in France, Mom," Pep told her.

"She means Paris, Texas, you dope!"

"Don't call your sister a dope," warned Dr. McDonald.

"Well, what's so special about Paris, Texas?" Pep asked.

"They have a replica of the Eiffel Tower there," Coke told her, "and it has a giant cowboy hat on top."

Dr. McDonald shook his head and closed his eyes for a moment, silently trying to compose the right words that would gently register his disapproval without provoking an argument.

"Y'know, it's not your birthday anymore, Bridge, and—" he began.

Even the twins knew those were the wrong words.

Go to Google Maps
(http://maps.google.com).

Click Get Directions.

In the A box, type
Denison TX.

In the B box, type
Paris TX.

Click Get Directions.

"Ben, I *told* you back in Virginia how badly I wanted to go to Paris, Texas," Mrs. McDonald said, her voice rising. "So don't act like it's a big surprise that I'm mentioning it now."

"Okay, okay!" said Dr. McDonald, defeated once again as he got back on the highway. "I've always wanted to see Paris."

Chapter 14

THIS IS WHY WE TRAVEL

Dr. McDonald hit the gas a little harder than necessary, because frustration needs to be expressed *somehow*, right? He followed Route 69 south for ten miles, and then merged onto Route 82 heading east. Paris, Texas, was a little more than an hour from Denison.

The twins pulled out magazines to help pass the time. Mrs. McDonald turned on the radio, fiddling with the buttons until she stopped at a country music station. Nobody in the family was a big fan of country music, but who could resist "My Wife Ran Off with

My Best Friend and I Sure Do Miss Him"?

In the middle of the song, the music suddenly stopped. A male voice came on and repeated a series of letters:

"P-C-F-T-H-B-L-R-N-Y-S-T-N."

There was a two-second pause, and then the voice said it again.

"P-C-F-T-H-B-L-R-N-Y-S-T-N."

Startled, Coke looked up from the magazine he had been reading. He recognized the voice. It was the same as the voice on the telephone the other night. It sounded vaguely computer generated. The voice repeated the letters.

"P-C-F-T-H-B-L-R-N-Y-S-T-N."

"It must be a broken record or something," said Mrs. McDonald.

"You'd think somebody at the radio station would notice," said Dr. McDonald. "Change the station, Bridge."

"Wait," said Coke.

He looked over at his sister. She nodded her head. Pep grabbed the little notepad she'd bought back in Memphis and quickly wrote the letters down.

On the radio, the song returned, and when it ended a new song came on—"If the Phone Don't Ring, You'll Know It's Me." Mrs. McDonald turned it up loud and began to sing along.

While their parents were occupied in the front seat, Coke and Pep put their heads together.

"That sounded just like the guy on the phone who told me to look under my pillow," Coke whispered to his sister.

"It's a cipher," Pep replied. "It has to be. They're coming at us over the radio now."

The twins looked at the letters Pep had written in her notepad: *P-C-F-T-H-B-L-R-N-Y-S-T-N.*

"Oh, come on," Coke said. "You gotta be kidding me. No way we're gonna figure *this* one out."

"You give up too easily," his sister told him.

Pep took the notepad and slid over to her side of the seat so she could concentrate. This one didn't look so hard. They had solved tougher ciphers before.

Pep tried all the usual strategies that had worked before, but none of them seemed to fit. That only made her more determined. Her forehead would wrinkle, and then she would brighten, and then her forehead would wrinkle again. The previous cipher had been easy. This was a hard one. After almost an hour, she still hadn't cracked it. She, too, was stumped.

Dr. McDonald pulled off the exit marked Paris. It looked like a pretty normal Texas town. Twenty-five thousand people. Forty-four square miles.

133

"Why is it called Paris?" Pep asked.

"It's probably in honor of Paris, France," her mother said, leafing through her guidebook.

"Actually, there are *fifteen* American towns named Paris," Coke said, having read that on a poster at school a long time ago.

I think you will agree, reader, that *nobody* should

know how many American towns are named Paris. It's just not information that needs to be retained.

Dr. McDonald drove through the east side of town until he reached the corner of Jefferson Road and South Collegiate Drive next to the LoveCivic Center.

"There it is!" Mrs. McDonald shouted, pointing. "Behold!"

And there it was—a dark metal structure that looked remarkably like the real Eiffel Tower, with the added attraction of having a ten-foot-wide red cowboy hat, slightly tilted at a jaunty angle, on top. Everybody got out of the car to get a better look.

"Well," said Dr. McDonald, "I must admit you don't see *that* every day."

"It's just like France," Pep said, "but in Texas."

"I can just about smell the baguettes baking," Coke said. "Oh, wait. That's probably just a cattle ranch."

"Think of it," Mrs. McDonald told the kids. "You're standing in the *only* place in the world that has a giant replica of the Eiffel Tower with a cowboy hat on it. This is why we travel, kids. To see things you can't see anywhere else."

"Do you think they have a fake Mona Lisa wearing a cowboy hat here too?" Coke asked.

Mrs. McDonald was used to her son's snarky remarks. She took out her camera to snap a few pictures, and also jotted down some notes for *Amazing but True*.

According to a plaque nearby, the fake Eiffel Tower was built in 1993 by volunteers. At first, the tower didn't have a cowboy hat on the top. But five years later, the town of Paris, Tennessee, built a fake Eiffel

Tower of its own that was five feet higher than the one in Paris, Texas. That's when the cowboy hat was added.

"Hey, take a picture of me with the tower in the background," Coke told his mother.

He went under the tower and struck a karate pose while Mrs. McDonald set up the shot.

"Take a step back," she instructed him.

He did, and as she was about to snap the picture, there was the sense that something out of the ordinary was about to happen. Everyone could feel it. Something was wrong. Something was happening. They just didn't know what it was.

A split second later, an object appeared in everyone's peripheral vision. The only person who didn't see it was Coke, who was posing for the camera.

"Watch out!" Pep screamed.

She bolted over and tackled her brother. They hit the ground together in a tangle of arms and legs.

"What the—"

At that instant, something smashed into the ground with a *boom* at the exact spot where Coke had been standing.

Well, it wasn't just *something*. It was a cow. A big, brown, 1,400-pound spotted cow.

As their parents rushed over, Coke and Pep looked

a few feet to their left to see the cow lying on the ground next to them. A very dead cow.

"It's a cow!" Coke said, stating the obvious. Then he peered up at the tower, struggling to see who would have been crazy enough to do such a thing.

"Are you okay?" Dr. McDonald asked, checking to see if there was any blood on his son in places where blood wasn't supposed to be.

"Yeah, I think so," Coke said, still dazed. Then he turned to his sister. "You saved my life."

"It was just instinct," she said. "I saw something falling. I didn't know what it was."

A few people came over to see what was going on. After all, it wasn't every day that a cow fell out of the fake Eiffel Tower. Some teenage girls took cell phone pictures of the cow and walked away giggling. A man wearing a cowboy hat and blue jeans walked over. He knelt down and put his hand on the cow.

"It's dead," he said.

"That's so sad," said Mrs. McDonald.

"It would have been a lot sadder if our kids were under it," Dr. McDonald told her.

"It's cold as an ice pop," said the guy in the cowboy hat, who appeared to know a thing or two about cows. "I reckon this bossy was dead before it hit the ground."

"Why would somebody drop a dead cow on my son's head?" Mrs. McDonald demanded. "For that matter, how did they get a dead cow up there in the first place?"

"Why is the sky blue?" the guy replied. "Why is sugar sweet? Stuff happens."

"Wait a minute," Dr. McDonald said, clearly annoyed. "There are scientific reasons why the sky is blue or sugar is sweet. There's no logical explanation for why a cow should fall on our son's head."

"Never said it was logical," drawled the guy in the cowboy hat. He stood up and walked away.

Just for the record, this was not the first time a large object had fallen—or been dropped—on the McDonald twins. Back in North Carolina, Pep was standing under a building that looked like a giant chest of drawers when a *real* chest of drawers fell out of it and nearly killed her. At South of the Border in South Carolina, Coke was standing under the giant Pedro statue when a bag full of plastic Pedro statues almost landed on him.

And now, a cow.

"Whoever did this is going to *pay*!" Coke said, his fists clenched.

He was sweating and his heart was racing, as you would imagine your heart might race if you had nearly been flattened by a dead cow dropped from sixty-five feet. Pep put her arm around him protectively.

"I'm sure it was just an accident," she said, shooting a look at her brother.

"Maybe we should take you to a doctor," Dr. McDonald told Coke.

"I'm fine. Let's just get out of here."

"Well, I want to file a formal complaint," said Mrs. McDonald. "Somebody should be notified that cows are falling on people. You could get killed out here. This place is dangerous."

While their parents went to look for a place to lodge their complaint, Pep walked her brother back to the car to rest and recuperate.

"Do you think that was intentional?" Pep asked.

"No, a dead cow *accidentally* fell out of that tower on my head," Coke snapped.

"You know what I mean. Did somebody drop it on purpose?"

"You can bet on it," Coke said, looking up again at the tower. "And he's gonna *pay*."

"Or she."

To get her mind off what had just happened, Pep opened her notepad and looked at the cipher that had been stumping her all morning:

P-C-F-T-H-B-L-R-N-Y-S-T-N

She stared at the message, manipulating the letters in her mind. And then, after a few minutes, Pep picked up a pencil. Her brain saw something it hadn't seen before. Maybe the adrenaline had something to do with it.

"I just noticed something," she told Coke. "There are no vowels."

"So?"

"Well, if there are no vowels, it's obvious," Pep told her brother. "All we need to do is put in the vowels."

"But how do we know where to put them?" Coke asked.

"The *TH* helps," Pep told him. "There's probably an *E* after that."

"How do you know?"

"Look at it," Pep said. "There aren't many words that have *THB* in them. And *THE* is a really common word. And if that word is *THE*, the next word is *BL-*something-*RNY*. What vowel would fit in there?"

"Only an *A*," Coke said. "*BLARNY*, or *BLARNEY*. The Blarney."

"The Blarney Stone!" Pep shouted. "*STN* must be *STONE* after you put the vowels in!"

"Then what would *PCF* mean?" Coke asked.

They both stared at the letters for a long time. . . .

PCF THE BLARNEY STONE

"Piece of!" Pep suddenly blurted out. "A piece of the Blarney Stone!"

"Wow, you are *good*."

"What's a blarney stone, anyway?" Pep asked.

"It's a big rock at the top of a castle in Blarney, Ireland," Coke explained, recalling a book he'd once read during detention. "They call it 'the Stone of Eloquence,' and the legend goes that if you kiss it, you'll never be lost for words."

"I don't get it," Pep said. "We're not going to Ireland. It doesn't make any sense."

Oh, it made sense. It just didn't make sense *yet*.

Go to Google Maps (http://maps.google.com).

Click Get Directions.

In the A box, type Paris TX.

In the B box, type Dallas TX.

Click Get Directions.

Chapter 15

X MARKS THE SPOT

If you recall from the first Genius Files book, Coke and Pep received a bunch of mysterious messages that appeared to have no common connection. But actually those messages led them to their climactic confrontation with Dr. Warsaw at The House on the Rock in Wisconsin.

In the second book, it also seemed as though the ciphers had nothing in common, but in the end they all referred to items inside the National Museum of American History, where the twins encountered the deranged teenager Archie Clone.

Once again, in the *third* book, the ciphers seemed to be completely incomprehensible, until the twins finally realized that they all had something to do with Graceland, Elvis Presley's mansion in Memphis, Tennessee. That's where Evil Elvis/Aunt Judy was waiting to ambush them.

But what could these two *new* messages possibly mean? Pep turned to a blank page in her notepad and wrote them out in her neat handwriting:

1. I WILL MEET YOU IN LLANO ESTACADO
2. A PIECE OF THE BLARNEY STONE

Dr. and Mrs. McDonald came back from the Lamar County Chamber of Commerce, where they had lodged a formal complaint about the dangerous conditions at the fake Eiffel Tower.

"What did you say?" Pep asked.

"I told them a dead cow fell out of the Eiffel Tower and almost landed on my son," said Dr. McDonald.

"And what did *they* say?" asked Pep.

"They just laughed," said Mrs. McDonald. "They thought it was funny."

It was, in an odd sort of way. After the family had gotten over the initial shock of what had happened, they were even able to joke about it.

"Hey, what has four legs and goes 'moo—thud'?" asked Pep.

"What?"

"A cow falling on Coke's head."

Back in the car, the McDonalds were heading south and west. It would be almost two hours to Dallas, mainly along I-30. They stopped for lunch at a little diner in Greenville, but the parents spent most of the time arguing over what they were going to do for the rest of the day.

"It says here that the first 7-Eleven opened in Dallas in 1927," said Mrs. McDonald. "But the Slurpee wasn't invented until fifty years later."

"Please don't tell me they have a Slurpee museum in Dallas," Dr. McDonald said, groaning. "I will have lost all faith in humanity."

"They don't, but at the Baylor University Medical Center, they have bronze-coated replicas of the hands of famous people like Louis Armstrong, Winston Churchill, Joe DiMaggio, and Walt Disney," Mrs. McDonald said. "That could be pretty interesting to see, don't you think?"

"Those could be *anybody's* hands in bronze," scoffed Dr. McDonald. "I don't need to see that."

"Hey, the world's largest patio chair is in Dallas!" Mrs. McDonald said more excitedly. "It's in front of a furniture store."

"I'm not driving to Dallas to look at a *chair*," Dr. McDonald said, "and that's final."

Listening to the two of them go at it was like watching two great tennis players whack a ball back and forth.

Coke and Pep's parents hardly ever fought back home, but they seemed to bicker a lot in the car. Maybe it had something to do with being so close together in a confined space, and having to make important decisions quickly.

In any case, Dr. and Mrs. McDonald finally hit on something they both wanted to see in Dallas—the Sixth Floor Museum.

"What's that?" asked Pep.

"The Sixth Floor Museum chronicles the assassination and legacy of John F. Kennedy," said her all-knowing brother.

You're probably aware that President Kennedy was gunned down in Dallas on November 22, 1963—a tragedy that shook the nation to its core. People who were alive that day remember exactly where they were when they heard the news that the president had been shot.

When they reached Dallas, Dr. McDonald drove up Elm Street on the western edge of the historic district downtown and parked the car behind an early 20th-century warehouse that used to be known as the

Texas School Book Depository. Shots rang out from the sixth floor of the building on that day in 1963. Today, the sixth and seventh floors are a museum jammed with exhibits about the assassination, and about Kennedy himself. Photography was not permitted in the museum, but Mrs. McDonald took notes for *Amazing but True*.

What the twins found most interesting was the window where the sniper's nest and rifle were found after the assassination. They could look out and see Dealey Plaza, where the president's motorcade passed. As Coke and Pep peered out that window, a guard informed them that there's an X painted on the street at the exact spot where the president was hit.

"I can't see the *X*," Coke said.

"That's because that tree is in the way," the guard told him.

"Well, if the tree is in the way, how could Lee Harvey Oswald *possibly* have shot the president from this window?" asked Coke, quite proud of himself for personally debunking the notion that Oswald was the lone gunman.

"The tree was a lot shorter in 1963," the guard informed him.

"Oh."

The museum was fascinating, but there was a lot

to absorb, and to the twins 1963 might as well have been ancient history. After an hour or so, they were ready to leave.

"I want to see *everything*," Dr. McDonald said. "This was one of the most important events in American history."

"Can we go outside and look at the *X* on the street?" asked Coke.

"Well, okay," their mother agreed reluctantly. "Meet us back at the car in an hour."

Coke and Pep took the stairs down and walked around the front of the building to Dealey Plaza. They weren't the only ones. A half-dozen tourists were mill-ing around the area with cameras and guidebooks. Invari-ably, they would look up to the sixth floor of the book deposi-tory building, and then down to the street.

"There it is," Coke said, pointing to the white X painted in the center lane.

"*That's* the exact spot where Kennedy was hit."

The twins walked over to the curb. Cars zipped down the street, many of them driving right over the X mark.

"Think about it," Pep said quietly. "If those bullets had missed by an inch, history would have been different. Kennedy would probably have been reelected and been president through 1968. Maybe he would have ended the war in Vietnam. Watergate would have never happened. Maybe—"

"You don't know any of that," Coke replied. "Nobody can know what would have happened if Kennedy had lived."

The traffic eased up. Coke looked up and down Elm Street. There were no cars.

"I want to stand on it," he said.

"It's just an *X*," said Pep.

"I know. I want to stand on the exact spot."

"It's a busy street," his sister warned. "You could get run over by a car."

"Who are you, Mom?" Coke asked. "Relax. Don't worry about it."

Elm is a one-way street, but Coke looked both ways just to be sure. Satisfied that there were no cars coming, he dashed out into the middle of the road.

"Be careful!" Pep yelled.

"I'm always careful!" Coke yelled back. "Look, I'm standing on it! This is the exact spot where the president was hit."

"Okay, you saw it," Pep yelled. "Come back now."

Coke glanced up and across the street for a moment to locate the window from which the shots had been fired. Then he looked down at the street.

"Hey, there's something written on the *X*," he said.

"What is it?"

Just as Coke was bending down to read the tiny letters in the *X*, two motorcycles came roaring around the bend on Elm Street.

"Coke, get out of the way!" his sister shouted.

He looked up. It was a three-lane road, but both of the motorcycles were in the center lane, and they were heading directly toward him at top speed. Their handlebars were nearly touching each other.

"What the—"

"The bowler dudes!" Pep screamed, pointing at the weird, bowler-shaped helmets the bikers were wearing.

The bowler dudes didn't look like they were going to veer around Coke. He couldn't jump to his left. He couldn't jump to his right. There was only one way to go.

Up.

Using the skills he had learned in his karate classes, Coke went from a deep crouch to pushing against the ground with all the energy he had to propel his body upward. He got pretty high—at least three feet in the air.

The bowler dudes, taken by surprise, reached out to grab Coke's legs as they passed, but missed him by inches. The rearview mirror of one of the bikes, however, caught on the bottom of Coke's T-shirt as he leaped.

As it passed by at close to fifty miles per hour, the mirror pulled at the shirt, flipping Coke around. His body did a 360 in the air and he landed roughly on his backside. The motorcycles kept right on going, roaring away down Elm Street.

Coke, dazed, still had the sense to crawl to the curb just before several cars came speeding down the street. His shirt was ripped and he was gasping for breath, but he seemed to be all right. Pep dragged him out of harm's way.

"Are you okay?" she asked.

"I think so," Coke said, still gasping for breath. "How could they know we were here? How did they know to come down the road at that moment?"

"They know things," Pep said. "And now *we* know that they're trying to kill us again. I *knew* we shouldn't have trusted them."

If Coke had jumped a millisecond earlier, or a millisecond later, he would have been hit by the motorcycles and surely killed. If his body had spun around a few miles per hour faster or slower, he would have landed on his head and very possibly been killed. If it hadn't been for these lucky breaks, it would have been the *second* assassination to take place at that exact same spot on Dealey Plaza in Dallas, Texas.

Chapter 16

HUB CITY

Did you ever have a really bad day when just about everything was going wrong? That was the kind of day Coke was having. So far, a cow had been dropped on him and he was almost run over by a couple of motorcycles. And it was still early afternoon.

There's a little hill on the north side of Elm Street in Dealey Plaza near some concrete steps. It's referred to as "the grassy knoll." Many Kennedy assassination experts believed at least one of the shots that hit the president came from this spot and *not* from the sixth floor of the Texas School Book Depository. Coke and Pep went over and sat down on this grassy knoll to regain their composure. They had about ten minutes until it was time to meet their parents in the parking lot.

"Are you going to be okay?" Pep asked.

"Yeah. I'm indestructible. You know that."

"That was a really dumb thing you did," Pep told her brother.

"I know."

Coke lay back on the grass, looking up at the sky. His T-shirt was ripped and his knees were scraped from crawling across the street.

"So . . . what did you see?" Pep asked him.

"Huh?"

"Just before those motorcycles came, you told me there was something written in the *X*," Pep reminded him. "What did it say?"

"Oh, yeah," Coke said. The near miss with the motorcycle had almost made him forget that he had bent down to look at the words on the street. "You're gonna laugh. It said *BUY ITCH.*"

"BUY ITCH?"

"It must be some kind of an ad," Coke said. "I guess

they're selling an anti-itch cream. Can you believe that? Companies will advertise *anywhere*, even in a place like this."

"Not necessarily," Pep replied. "Maybe *BUY ITCH* is an anagram that we're supposed to figure out."

"Are you serious?" Coke said, sitting up. "You think somebody would send us a cipher by putting letters on an *X* in the middle of the street?"

"Why not?" Pep said. "They put one at the bottom of a swimming pool, remember? They put one on the radio. When we were in Chicago, they put one on the scoreboard at Wrigley Field!"

"But what could *BUY ITCH* mean?" Coke asked, as he juggled the letters around in his head.

Pep took her notepad and pencil from her pocket and wrote *BUY ITCH* at the top of a page. Then she got to work, writing down every possible combination of those letters.

"CUT BY HI," she said softly as she wrote. "No, that can't be it. *I CUB THY* . . . *CHIT BUY* . . ."

It was just nonsense words. It didn't seem like *BUY ITCH* could possibly mean anything besides *BUY ITCH*. Coke looked up at the passing cars, while his sister continued working on new letter combinations in her head.

"Wait a minute!" she said suddenly. "I think I've *got* it!"

She wrote this on her pad:

HUB CITY

"Hub City?"

"'Hub City' is an anagram for *BUY ITCH*!" she told her brother. "We need to go to Hub City."

"Oh, great," Coke said. "Now all we have to do is find out where Hub City is."

When the twins met their parents in the parking lot, Mrs. McDonald took one look at Coke and went into "Mom Mode."

"What happened to your shirt?" she asked.

"It ripped."

"I can *see* that!" said Mrs. McDonald. "How did it rip? I left you on your own for less than an hour, and now you look like you got run over by a truck."

"Funny you should say that, Mom," Coke told her. "You see, I was standing on the *X* in the street where President Kennedy was shot when these two motor-cycles came out of nowhere and almost ran me over.

So I jumped up in the air and flipped around, and—"

"Ha-ha! That's a good one, son," said Dr. McDonald. "How do you come up with this stuff?"

"I guess I just have a vivid imagination, Dad."

They got in the car and Dr. McDonald paid the parking attendant. But Mrs. McDonald wasn't finished nagging Coke.

"I wish you would take better care of your clothes," she told him. "We just bought that shirt the other day, and now it's ruined."

"I'll try, Mom," said Coke, who knew from experience that it was always better to agree with his mother than to argue with her.

They got back on the road and after a few minutes everyone had calmed down a little.

"Can we borrow your computer, Mom?" asked Pep. "We need to look something up."

"What for, sweetie?" Mrs. McDonald said from the front seat.

"It's an assignment for school," said Coke, who was always the better liar of the two.

"You're working on schoolwork over summer vacation?" Dr. McDonald asked, turning around so he could see it with his own eyes. "Are you feeling okay?"

Mrs. McDonald handed her laptop back, warning the kids to be careful with it because her entire website—her entire *career*—was stored in that little box. Then she turned the radio back on. "How Can I Miss You If You Won't Go Away" was playing, and Dr. McDonald turned it up loud.

Coke took the laptop and Googled "Hub City." In 0.19 seconds, he had 125,000 results. He clicked the first one on the list.

"It says Hub City is a manufacturer of worm gear," he whispered to his sister.

"What's worm gear?" Pep asked. "Clothing for worms?"

"It has something to do with motors," Coke explained.

Coke scrolled down to see some of the other results for "Hub City." He hoped that the search would turn up the name of a city with that nickname. Unfortunately, the top search results included the name of a hockey club in Boston, a drag racing track in Mississippi, a bicycle store in Maryland, a Ford dealership in Louisiana, and a brewery in Iowa.

"There's no way of knowing which Hub City is *our* Hub City," Pep said. "It's another dead end."

As frustrated as she was, Pep was a chronic list maker, and she dutifully added the new message to her list in the notepad. . . .

I. I WILL MEET YOU IN LLANO ESTACADO
2. A PIECE OF THE BLARNEY STONE

3. HUB CITY

There was still no obvious connection between the items, no clear thread that tied them all together. But after what had happened to her brother in Paris and Dallas, one thing was increasingly clear—someone was out to harm them . . . again.

Go to Google Maps (http://maps.google.com).

Click Get Directions.

In the A box, type Dallas TX.

In the B box, type Arlington TX.

Click Get Directions.

Chapter 17

FRAMED

Interstate 30, which starts in Little Rock, Arkansas, stretches west over 350 miles, across Texas. In the Dallas area it's known as the Tom Landry Highway, in honor of the longtime coach of the Dallas Cowboys. The McDonalds were only on the road for fifteen minutes when they pulled off at the exit marked ARLINGTON.

"Why are we stopping *here*?" Pep asked.

"You'll see," said Mrs. McDonald. "It's a surprise."

"I don't like surprises," Coke said, rubbing his bruised knee. He'd already had enough surprises for the day.

"Oh, you'll like this one," his mother assured him.

The twins looked around anxiously as Dr. McDonald pulled off the highway on the right and merged onto Six Flags Road.

"We're going to Six Flags!" Pep shouted excitedly. "We're going to Six Flags!"

Six Flags, as you probably know, is a popular amusement park chain. There are nineteen of them in North America. The twins had been to Six Flags Discovery Kingdom back home in California, and they could barely contain their enthusiasm.

"I hate to break it to you," Mrs. McDonald said, "but we're *not* going to Six Flags."

"Why not?" asked Pep, deflated.

"Where are we going, then?" Coke asked as they drove right past the sign for SIX FLAGS OVER TEXAS. Another sign pointed toward RANGERS BALLPARK.

"Are we going to a Rangers game?" Pep asked.

"No . . . ," Mrs. McDonald said mysteriously.

The car pulled into a parking lot. A large office building in the distance had a sign in big letters on it: USBC.

"What's that?" Pep asked.

There was no need to answer, because as they got closer Pep could see what the letters stood for—United States Bowling Congress.

Other signs indicated the International Bowling Museum and Hall of Fame, the International Bowling Campus, and the International Bowling Training and Research Center. It was all part of a giant bowling complex.

"You gotta be kidding me," Coke said. "They do

bowling research? You roll a ball down an alley and try to knock down pins. What is there to *research*?"

"Keep an open mind, son," said Dr. McDonald. "I think you're going to like this."

"I'd rather go to Six Flags," Coke grumbled.

They parked near a giant white bowling pin and Mrs. McDonald bought tickets for the bowling museum.

Everything has a history. If you take any object, any activity, any sport, there was somebody who invented it a long time ago. Somebody else probably improved it or perfected it. A third person may have made it into something that millions of people use or do every day. And if we personally are interested in that thing, we want to know more about it. That's why there are museums devoted to yo-yos, mustard, Spam, gourds, rock and roll, spies, and yes, bowling.

The place was enormous, and even the twins found the displays to be interesting. Who knew that primitive bowling pins were found in an Egyptian tomb that was dated 3200 BCE? Who knew that ninety-five million people around the world bowl, in ninety different countries? The museum was filled with information and interactive exhibits that explained just about everything you always wanted to know about bowling but never thought to ask.

Even so, after a while Coke and Pep were a bit tired of reading about it and ready to do some actual bowling.

"Can Pep and I blow this pop stand while you guys finish the museum?" Coke asked his parents.

They agreed, and found out that there was open bowling across the street at the International Bowling Training and Research Center. The twins had no trouble finding it, and there weren't that many people on the lanes in the late afternoon.

Coke and Pep went to the front desk, which was raised a few feet above the floor. A woman was behind the desk, and when she turned around to face them, the twins shrank back in terror.

"Mrs. Higgins!"

"If it isn't the McDonald twins!" she said cheerfully. "Are you two stalking me or something?"

Who would have thought that their psychotic health teacher would now be working at the International Bowling Training and Research Center?

Pep instinctively started to run, but Coke held her back. He remembered that the last time they had encountered Mrs. Higgins, she hadn't laid a hand on them. She had even been *nice* to them and their parents. Maybe she had truly been rehabilitated.

"What are you doing here?" he asked. "I thought you were working at the Bauxite Museum. It was just a few days ago."

"I quit," she replied. "I decided that bauxite was boring. I wanted to devote my life to something more exciting."

"Bowling?" asked Coke.

"It's a trick," Pep said. "Don't fall for it."

"Bowling is the only pure sport," Mrs. Higgins said, a rapturous smile filling her face. "It's just you against the pins. They stand, or they fall. There's no in-between. No interpretation of the rules. No instant replay. No referee or umpire is necessary. It's pure . . . magic."

"I never thought of bowling that way," admitted Coke.

"And we have some of the most innovative and cutting-edge coaching technologies available in the bowling industry today," Mrs. Higgins told the twins. "High-speed video cameras, motion-capture devices, foot-pressure sensors. Anyway, what size do you kids wear?"

"What size of what?"

"Bowling shoes, of course," she said. "You can't bowl without bowling shoes."

"Oh, yeah."

The twins told her their shoe sizes and she handed them each a pair of bowling shoes.

"Lane three," Mrs. Higgins told them. "Have fun!"

The twins put the shoes on and went to look for bowling balls.

"I really think she's changed," Coke said. "She's really into bowling. You can see it in her eyes. She's not going to bother us anymore."

"I don't have a good feeling about this," Pep said. "It can't be just a coincidence that she gets a job wherever *we* happen to be."

"You think too much," Coke said as he picked up a ball that felt good in his hands. "That's your problem. Just try to have a little fun for a change."

They each found a ball to their liking, and they brought the balls over to lane three. Pep punched their names into the computer, letting her brother go first. He was a good bowler, once scoring a 203 at a

friend's birthday party.

"Watch and learn," Coke said as he prepared to make his first roll.

He eyed the pins, made a smooth five-step approach to the line, and let the ball go.

Gutter ball.

"Ha!" Pep shouted. "Loser!"

"I'm just getting warmed up," Coke replied as he waited for his ball to come back.

Actually, he was suddenly feeling overheated. Coke held his hand over the blower for a moment to dry off the sweat. Then he picked up his ball, aimed more carefully . . . and threw *another* gutter ball.

"Oh man!" Pep shouted, jumping up to take her turn. "You are *pathetic!*"

Pep wasn't much better, knocking down three pins on her first roll and one on her second. But she had never been a very good bowler. Now, at least, she was ahead by four pins.

As Pep was throwing her second ball, Coke tried to think of the last time he threw two gutter balls in a row. Probably when he was in second grade, he thought. First grade, maybe. He was anxious to redeem himself in the second frame. He was better than this.

"The ball feels so heavy," he said as he picked it up.

"No excuses, loser," his sister shouted. "I am *crushing* you."

Coke rolled the ball down the alley, but his heart wasn't in it. After the ball slid into the right gutter three-quarters of the way down the alley, he sat down on the bench heavily. He was perspiring.

"I don't feel so good," he told Pep.

"Me neither," she said. "I feel really tired, like I'm going to pass out."

She threw a couple of weak gutter balls and then plopped down on the bench next to her brother.

"I don't know what's the matter," Coke admitted. "This *never* happens to me. I can barely raise my arm."

At that point, Mrs. Higgins strolled over, a jaunty spring in her step.

"How are you kids doing?" she asked cheerfully. "Having fun?"

"Not so much," Coke said slowly, his eyes half closed. "We're sick. It must have been . . . something we ate for lunch."

"Oh, I don't think that was it," said Mrs. Higgins. "It was probably the poison I put in your bowling shoes."

It took a moment to register what she had just said. Coke's and Pep's brains seemed to be working in slow motion.

"Did you just say you put poison . . . in our bowling shoes?" Coke asked wearily.

"Yes, it looks just like talcum powder," Mrs. Higgins replied matter-of-factly. "It will take a few minutes for it to be fully absorbed into your system. The skin on the feet is very thick. It's not the best way to deliver poison."

"That's not a very . . . nice thing to do," Pep said drowsily. "Why would you . . . put poison in our bowling shoes?"

"How *else* could I get you to take the poison, silly?" asked Mrs. Higgins. "You can't just hand somebody a poison pill and expect 'em to take it *willingly*."

Fighting to keep his eyes open, Coke let out a little involuntary laugh.

"You . . . poisoned us . . . through our bowling shoes," he mumbled. "What a . . . brilliant idea."

"Well, I thought about sprinkling the poison on a pizza and bringing it over to you," said Mrs. Higgins, "but I didn't think you'd trust me enough to eat it."

"Are we going to . . . die?" Pep asked, putting her head down on the bench.

"Of course not," Mrs. Higgins said. "You're just going to sleep for a while. Once you're unconscious, I can do anything I want to you."

"Didn't you tell us . . . you weren't going to hurt kids

anymore?" Pep said, yawning. "You said you were going to be . . . nice."

"Oh, yeah," Mrs. Higgins said with a chuckle. "That was what's called *lying.*"

"I can't believe we let you fool us . . . again," Coke said, resting his head on the floor next to his sister.

"Yes, I'm pretty good at that," Mrs. Higgins said. "Always have been. When I was in high school, I was voted Most Likely to Mislead. And look at me now. I can stare you right in the face and say one thing while meaning the exact opposite thing. Not many people can pull that off. It's my gift."

But the twins didn't hear any of it. They were unconscious.

Chapter 18
A NEW SPORT

When he opened his eyes, Coke was sprawled across lane two, his head and feet in the gutters, about ten feet in front of the pins. Pep was in the same position, lying across lane three.

But neither of them knew that yet, because except for a few pinpoints of light, they were in total darkness. Somebody had taken off the poisoned bowling shoes and put their sneakers back on their feet.

"Where are we?" Coke asked his sister. "What time is it?"

"How should I know?" she replied. "Mrs. Higgins

probably kidnapped us and put us in a cell while she decides what to do to us next."

"How could we have been so *stupid*?" he said. "I can't believe we ever trusted her."

"We?" Pep replied. *"I* didn't trust her. *You* trusted her. I tried to run away as soon as I saw her face. You stopped me, remember?"

"There's no point in arguing about it now," Coke said.

"There's no point in arguing about it because I'm *right*," Pep replied angrily. "You have no argument."

Actually, there was no point in arguing about it for another reason—they were about to be attacked.

At the far end of lanes two and three, two men silently picked up bowling balls and got into position to bowl.

Suddenly, all the lights in the International Bowling Training and Research Center flashed on.

"What the—" Coke said, looking up.

"I hear something," Pep said, her voice cracking. "What's that sound?"

It was the distinctive sound of a fifteen-pound bowling ball hitting the wood floor and rolling down an alley. Two bowling balls, to be precise. They were rolling down lanes two and three.

"Watch out!" Coke shouted to his sister.

"Ahhhhhhhhhh!" she screamed.

One of the balls was coming on a direct line toward Pep's head. The other one was about to hit Coke in the midsection. At the last possible instant, both twins flopped out of the way and narrowly avoided getting slammed. The balls passed harmlessly by, knocking down some of the pins behind them. The two men at the other end of lanes two and three had already picked up new balls and were preparing to heave them.

"Stop!" Pep shouted uselessly. "Are you crazy?"

"They're not crazy! They're trying to kill us!" Coke said.

"Who are they?"

"Who do you think? The bowler dudes!"

Yes, the bowler dudes. The two mentally challenged lunatics, who had been terrorizing the twins from the very beginning, were at it again.

"Ha-ha-ha-ha!" cackled the bowler dude with the mustache. "This is fun!"

He let loose with his second ball. Pep stumbled while trying to get up to dodge it and almost got hit in the ankle. Coke jumped up at the last instant and the clean-shaven bowler dude's ball passed right beneath him.

"You like bowling?" shouted Mrs. Higgins from the front desk. "Let's see if you like it from the *pin's* point of view!"

"We gotta get out of here!" Coke shouted, reaching over to grab Pep by the hand and pull her up. The bowler dudes had already picked up balls from the ball return.

"Where are we going to go?" Pep yelled.

"Over there!" Coke shouted, pointing to the far corner of the large building. "There's a fire exit! Follow me!"

The twins, still feeling the effects of the poison that had been put in their bowling shoes, struggled get their footing on the slippery surface. Gingerly, they stepped over the gutter of lane three and hopped onto lane four.

The bowler dudes, watching them carefully, moved over to lane four, both heaving balls down that alley at the same time.

"Jump, Pep!" Coke shouted.

They both jumped and narrowly evaded the balls.

"Ooooh, I almost got a strike that time!" one of the bowler dudes shouted gleefully.

"You need to work on your follow-through," his brother cackled as he picked up another ball.

As the McDonald twins frantically scampered

across lanes five and six, the bowler dudes moved across the floor with them, picking up balls and whipping them down the alley as fast as they could roll them.

"Watch your left!" Coke shouted as he ran across lane seven. Pep dodged that ball, and the next one too.

As the twins dashed from lane to lane, the bowler dudes ran across the floor, chucking shot after shot at them. It was as though Coke and Pep were being attacked with cannonballs.

"This is much more fun than aiming at pins," the mustachioed bowler dude said as he ran from lane nine to lane ten to let loose his next shot.

"Yeah," said his clean-shaven brother, already at lane twelve. "It adds a human dimension to the game."

"Hey, we invented a new sport!" the mustachioed bowler dude said, racing to pick up the next ball. "This should be in the Olympics! Ha-ha-ha-ha!"

"Stop fooling around, you idiots!" shouted Mrs. Higgins from the front desk. "Knock them over! That's what I'm paying you for! Quick! They're getting away!"

Coke and Pep managed to make it to lane nineteen without getting hit with more than a glancing blow. Coke was the first one to reach the emergency exit.

He ignored the warning on the door and pushed hard on the handle, which set off an alarm. But at least the door opened, and Coke and Pep dashed through it and out into the parking lot.

It took a few minutes to find their parents, who had just come out of the International Bowling Museum and were walking back to the car.

"Did you kids have fun?" asked Mrs. McDonald. "I got you a souvenir—a bowling pin refrigerator magnet."

"Let's go!" Coke shouted breathlessly when he reached the car. He was panting and sweating, and his hair was all messed up.

"Look at you two," Dr. McDonald said with a laugh. "Were you bowling, or playing ice hockey?"

"It's a long story," Pep said, getting in the car and flopping onto the rear seat.

"I had no idea that bowling could get so physical," marveled Mrs. McDonald.

Go to Google Maps (http://maps.google.com).

Click Get Directions.

In the A box, type Arlington TX.

In the B box, type Mineral Springs TX.

Click Get Directions.

Chapter 19

SPIN CYCLE

Coke and Pep weren't laughing. There was no doubt anymore. Something had happened. Something had changed. Mrs. Higgins and the bowler dudes were out to get them again. Maybe Dr. Warsaw had recovered from his meltdown and decided to resume his quest to eliminate them. Whatever had happened, their lives were obviously in danger.

It had been a *long* day. The twins weren't in any mood to make chitchat in the car. Dr. McDonald pulled into a drive-through joint for burgers and then got back on the road, heading west on I-30 from Arlington. His plan was to get on I-35 and stop somewhere at a motel for the night.

Mrs. McDonald was looking through her guidebook, as usual. Just as they were about to pull off I-30 at the exit for I-35, she shouted, "Ben, stop the car!"

Dr. McDonald slammed on the brakes and pulled over to the shoulder of the road. Fortunately, everyone had a seat belt on. They were all getting used to this kind of thing.

"What is it?"

"We have to go to the washing machine museum!"

"Are you out of your mind?" Dr. McDonald shouted at his wife. "I almost caused a huge accident just then! You could have gotten us all killed!"

"I had to stop you before you took the exit," Mrs. McDonald explained. "My readers would never forgive me if I didn't tell them about the washing machine museum."

"There's *really* a museum devoted to washing machines?" Pep asked.

Coke just shook his head. Nothing surprised him anymore. Dr. McDonald let out a sigh.

"Where is it?" he asked.

"Mineral Wells," Mrs. McDonald replied. "It's only an hour west of here."

"Bridge, it's been a *long* day . . ."

"That's for sure," Coke said.

". . . and now you're asking me to drive an hour out of the way—to go to a museum about *washing machines*?"

"It's free, Ben," said Mrs. McDonald.

"Of *course* it's free!" he exploded. "Nobody wants to go there. Nobody's going to pay good money to look at a bunch of old washing machines! I wouldn't go if they paid me."

"You don't understand, Ben," said Mrs. McDonald gently. "The museum is just a part of a regular laundromat. All the clothes we bought back in Memphis are dirty now. We've got to do a load of wash anyway. We might as well do it at the washing machine museum."

Dr. McDonald took a minute, closing his eyes. Bridget McDonald was a wonderful woman. She was bright, funny, dedicated, and beautiful. But she wasn't easy to be married to.

"Okay, okay," he finally grumbled.

Instead of turning off at the exit, Dr. McDonald continued west on I-30. Shortly after passing a small airport, the road split and he got on Route 180, which goes directly to Mineral Wells. Route 180 is also called West Hubbard Street, which happens to be the street where the Laumdronat is located.

Yes, that's how it's supposed to be spelled—Laum-dronat.

It was a plain white building. Dr. McDonald found a parking spot down the street and popped open the trunk. The rest of the family gathered up their dirty clothes.

"I can't believe we're going to a washing machine museum," Pep said as they opened the door.

Laumdronat is essentially a regular laundromat that has a display of vintage washing machines. On a shelf above the modern machines are old-time tubs, washboards, and laundry accessories dating back to the days before most homes had electricity. Hanging from the ceiling are some ironing boards. There are also signs that say LAUNDRY, which are, for some reason, upside down.

"It's the history of laundry!" Mrs. McDonald enthused. "Isn't this fascinating?"

No, was the unanimous silent response from the rest of the family.

"Believe it or not, there's *another* washing machine museum, in Colorado," she told them.

"If we have to go there," said Dr. McDonald, "I'll shoot myself."

"Oh, you people are no fun at all," Mrs. McDonald

179

said as she began separating the darks from the lights.

A few other people were doing their wash, but there were plenty of machines available. Once the clothes were inside and swishing around, Mrs. McDonald started taking pictures and jotting down notes for *Amazing but True*. There were a couple of ancient Pac-Man games in the corner, and Coke dug some quarters out of his pocket so he and Pep could play. Dr. McDonald pulled up a chair and read his newspaper to kill time. The dryers were huge, so when the clothes were done washing, Mrs. McDonald was able to fit all the darks and lights into one machine.

When the dryer clicked off, everyone helped to fold and carry the clothes out to the car. They were about to drive away when—

"Dad!" Coke yelled. "Stop!"

"What *now*?"

"I'm missing a pair of my underwear."

"Well, go get it," his father said wearily.

Coke hopped out of the car and ran back inside the Laumdronat. It was empty now. He went over to the dryer they had been using and looked through the round window. Spinning around in there were his missing Fruit of the Looms. He opened the door.

As he leaned inside to grab the underwear, Coke was taken by surprise. The two bowler dudes came

out of nowhere, shoved him from behind, and pushed him headfirst into the dryer.

"What the—"

See? I *told* you that Coke would be shoved into a spinning clothes dryer! You just had to be a little patient.

The dryer door slammed behind him, and then the whole world began to spin.

"Stop!" Coke yelled as his body spun around. "Ouch! Let me out!"

The dryer was spinning fast, but not fast enough for the centrifugal force to hold Coke's body against the inside of the drum. He tumbled around until he reached the top, and then he fell to the bottom with a thud.

"Ooof!" he grunted. "Oww! Turn it off! *Helllllp!*"

As he spun around, Coke caught a glimpse of the two bowler dudes, their smiling faces pressed against the round window. He could hear their cackling laughter as they held the dryer door closed.

Within seconds, Coke started to feel dizzy from the spinning, and he realized he had to do something quickly or he would lose consciousness in there. If that happened and his head were to bang hard against the drum, it could be all over for him.

As he spun around and around, he got himself into position, gathered up the strength he had left, and slammed his right foot against the door the same way he had been taught to kick in karate class. The door flew open and the machine slowed to a stop.

Coke climbed out of the opening and fell on the floor. He tried to look around, but the world was still spinning. By the time he was able to see clearly, the bowler dudes were out the front door and running down the street.

Coke struggled to his feet and walked unsteadily back to the car.

"What took you?" asked Pep. "I was worried about you. How long does it take to get a pair of underwear out of a dryer, anyway?"

"I went for a spin," Coke replied.

All in all, it had been one lousy day. In fact, it may have been one of the worst days the McDonald twins had ever experienced.

Coke thought about everything that had happened to him since he woke up that morning. He had nearly been run over by two motorcycles. His shoes had been poisoned. He had been attacked by maniacs with bowling balls. And he had been pushed into a spinning clothes dryer. It was amazing that he was still alive.

Oh, and a cow had nearly fallen on his head. He'd almost forgotten.

Dr. McDonald drove east on Hubbard Street until he passed the Budget Host Mesa Motel near Lake Mineral Wells State Park. It was late, and the vacancy sign was blinking. He pulled in and got two rooms.

Wearily, the twins brushed their teeth and laid out the clean clothes they would wear the next day. As Coke picked up the Fruit of the Looms he had retrieved from the back of the dryer, he noticed something unusual. There were some letters written inside the waistband—letters that had not been there before. . . .

QBUXPOXKDBO

"Oh no," he said to his sister, "guess what?"

"What?"

"We got another one," he told her.

But both of the twins were too tired, too sore, and too frustrated to even think about solving the cipher. They crawled into their beds and went to sleep.

Go to Google Maps (http://maps.google.com).

Click Get Directions.

In the A box, type Mineral Wells TX.

In the B box, type Waco TX.

Click Get Directions.

When he woke up on the morning of July 16, Coke felt sore all over, but a little better in his head. There's something about getting a good night's sleep that helps to put yesterday behind you.

The McDonald family got back on the road. Route 180 headed east and merged with I-20. From there, it was a straight shot south on I-35 all the way to Waco, Texas. It doesn't sound like much, but it was a long drive, over two hours.

Most drives in Texas *are* long drives. It takes about

twelve hours to cross the state. That's with no rest stops. About 740 miles. Do you know how long it takes to drive the highway across the middle of New Jersey? Forty-five minutes. About forty miles. Don't believe me? Look it up.

Of course, the speed limit in some parts of Texas is over *eighty* miles per hour. And forget about driving the speed limit. If you drive the speed limit in Texas, the other cars will be all over your back bumper like cheese on macaroni. Dr. McDonald liked driving fast, and now he had a car that liked it just as much as he did.

Pep pulled out her notepad to work on the latest cipher. She felt a renewed urgency now. Somebody was out to get them. Her brother's skills were effective, but they weren't enough. She would have to use her wits to survive. Solving the cipher could be the key.

While their parents were flipping around the radio stations in the front seat, Pep took the letters *QBUX-POXKDBO* and did just about everything she could do to crack the code. She looked at the letters backward. Upside-down. Sideways.

QBUXPOXKDBO

"Oh man!" Coke said as he looked over her shoulder.

"That looks *impossible*."

"You're intimidated by the *Q* and the *X*s," Pep told him. "It doesn't matter what the letters are. They just represent other letters. Let's break it down. Eleven letters. This is probably two words, maybe three."

"So?"

"The only letters that appear twice are the two *X*s and two *B*s, see?" she continued. "So they very possibly represent *E* and *A*."

"Why do you say that?" Coke asked.

"Because *E* and *A* are two of the most commonly used letters," Pep replied.

She studied the cipher for a long time, occasionally furrowing her brow or wrinkling up her nose as she worked on it silently.

"I can almost see the wheels turning in your head," Coke said as he watched her.

Pep stopped for a moment.

"That gives me an idea!" she said as she turned to a clean page in her notepad and drew a circle. "This could be a shift cipher."

"Shift cipher?" her brother asked. "What does that mean?"

Pep didn't bother answering. Instead, she wrote the letters of the alphabet around the circle, going clockwise.

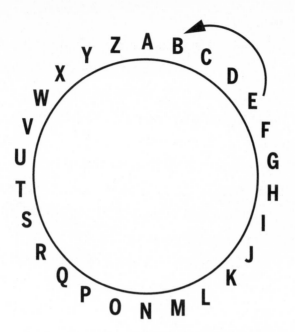

"You shift all the letters of the alphabet by a fixed amount," Pep explained. "Back in Roman times, that's what Julius Caesar did to keep his messages secret."

"How can you possibly know that?" Coke asked his sister.

"I know some stuff, and you know some stuff," Pep replied. "Look. Let's say the two *B*s are actually *E*s. That would mean that all the letters have been shifted counterclockwise by two. And if that's true, the two *X*s are *A*s."

Pep wrote the cipher out again, with the new letters. . . .

QEUAPOAKDEO

"That doesn't help much," Coke remarked.

"No," Pep said, "but it might if we shift *all* the letters counterclockwise by two."

With that logic, the *Q* became a *T*, the *U* became an *X*, and the *P* became an S. Pep wrote them down.

"Texas!" Coke said. "*QBUXP* is Texas!"

"And *OXKDBO* is . . . ," Pep said as she tackled the rest of the letters one at a time, "*R-A-N-G-E-R*! Texas Ranger! That's a baseball team, right?"

"It's also a law enforcement agency," Coke told her. "They investigate crime and stuff. But what does that have to do with the other clues we got—the piece of the Blarney Stone, or Hub City, or anything?"

"Beats me," Pep admitted glumly. "Can't help you there."

Dutifully, she wrote out the clues they had so far:

1. I WILL MEET YOU IN LLANO ESTACADO
2. A PIECE OF THE BLARNEY STONE
3. HUB CITY
4. TEXAS RANGER

The Ferrari approached the outskirts of Waco. The city is on the Brazos River and was first settled by the Huaco Indians. You would not call it a small town.

The population is over 124,000.

"Did you know that Dr Pepper was invented in Waco in 1885?" Mrs. McDonald reported from the front seat.

"Oh no," Coke grumbled. "Please don't tell me there's a Dr Pepper Museum."

"There's a Dr Pepper Museum," his mother replied.

"I *told* you not to tell me that."

"If we had a third child, we would have named her Pepper," Dr. McDonald chimed in from the driver's seat.

"What if she was a boy?" Pep asked.

"We would have named *him* Pepper," Dr. McDonald replied. "Boys can be called Pepper. There used to be a baseball player on the St. Louis Cardinals named Pepper Martin."

Just northwest of the city, he pulled off the interstate and drove a few short miles until he reached a parking lot for something called the Waco Mammoth Site.

"What is *this*?" Pep asked.

"You'll find out," Mrs. McDonald said, knowing full well that if she *told* the twins what it was, they would come up with every possible reason not to get out of the car.

The Waco Mammoth Site proved to be fascinating for everyone. In 1978, at this spot on the Bosque River,

two men stumbled upon a large bone sticking out of a ravine. It turned out to be part of the skeleton of a 68,000-year-old mammoth. Not only that, but fifteen other mammoths were scattered under the earth at the same location.

A lost world had been discovered. Soon, people started coming from all over to see the partly dug-up bones. The site was turned into a tourist attraction, complete with a scenic trail, a welcome center, and the inevitable gift shop.

While their parents waited in line for the guided tour, Coke and Pep scampered ahead onto the suspended walkway over the mammoth bones.

"Think of it," Coke said as he leaned over the rail to peer at the tusks and bones below. "They all died right here, at the same time. They probably drowned in a flash flood or something."

"It's kinda gross," Pep said. "I mean, what if those bones were human bones?"

"They weren't humans," her brother replied. "So it's not gross."

Old people are forced to confront their mortality on a daily basis. Children, for the most part, don't have to.

Death is so far away. You have your whole lifetime ahead of you.

For children like Coke and Pepsi McDonald, however, it was a different story. In the past few weeks, they had been tortured with extreme cold, heat, noise, electricity, and fire. They had jumped off a cliff. They had been attacked with everything from motorcycles to bowling balls. And yet they were still alive.

"I wouldn't want to die like those mammoths," Pep said solemnly as she looked down at the large bones.

At that moment, a trapdoor opened in the walkway and the twins tumbled into the darkness of the bone-yard below.

Chapter 21

THANKS FOR NOTHING

"**H**ow *would* you like to die?" asked a voice in the dark.

Pep went to scream, but a hand came up to cover her mouth before she got a sound out.

Coke struggled to his feet, only to be grabbed from behind by powerful arms.

"Shhhhhhhh!" a voice said. "It's *us*."

The twins turned around to see who had grabbed them.

"Bones!"

"Mya!"

The pair were dressed in tan uniforms with name

tags that said ARCHAEOLOGIST, WACO MAMMOTH SITE.

"What are *you* doing here?" the twins asked simultaneously.

"We needed to speak with you," Mya told them.

"We have reason to believe that your lives are in danger once again," said Bones.

"Gee, ya *think*?" Coke said sarcastically. "Yesterday somebody dropped a dead cow on my head. And then I was attacked with motorcycles and bowling balls."

"Who's after us *now*?" Pep asked.

"I'm sorry to say it's Dr. Warsaw again," Bones replied.

"That's impossible," Coke said. "We saw him in Hot Springs. He was a wreck. He tried to kill us in the vapor cabinets, but he couldn't bring himself to do it. He had some kind of a mental breakdown right in front of us."

"It's not Dr. Warsaw *himself* that we're worried about," Mya said. "We think he may have created a clone."

"What?!?" Coke said. "How is that possible? I thought human cloning was *years* away."

"It *was* years away," Bones told him. "But that was years ago when they said it was years away. Now those years have passed. It's now. And it's possible."

"You mean to say that now there are *two* Dr. Warsaws?" asked Pep.

193

"We don't have proof," Mya said, "only our suspicions. We've heard rumors."

Coke kicked at the dirt, nearly breaking his foot on a mammoth tusk.

"Well, this is just *great*," he said disgustedly. "That *doubles* the chances that he's going to get us."

Pep could see her brother's emotions were getting the best of him. That wasn't a good thing. He would be useless in an emergency if he couldn't control himself.

"We've been getting these secret messages," Pep said, trying to change the subject. "Hub City . . . Texas Ranger . . . a piece of the Blarney Stone. Do you know who is sending them?"

"No," Mya said. "But I'll look into it."

"Are you two good for *anything*?" Coke spat. "All you ever do is sneak around with your funny disguises and pop up out of nowhere to scare the crap out of us. Then you bring us bad news. You never help us."

Bones took a step back. He wasn't used to being talked to that way.

"Coke, stop," Pep said.

"Need I remind you that *we* were the ones who saved your lives when you had to jump off the cliff in California?" Bones said calmly. "And we spent our annual budget to get you a Frisbee grenade, which you threw into a swimming pool."

"My sister used it to knock the gun out of Evil Elvis's hand!" Coke said. "It *ricocheted* into the swimming pool!"

Coke was furious. It looked as though he was going to throw a punch at Bones, but Mya stepped between them.

"Let's not argue, guys," she said. "We're sincerely trying to help you. Here, I brought you a little present."

She took something out of her pocket and handed it to Coke. It was a refrigerator magnet in the shape of Texas. He looked at it carefully.

"Is it a camera?" he asked. "Where's the lens?"

"It's not a camera," Mya said. "You put it on your refrigerator."

"And it explodes?" Coke asked hopefully. "Why would I want to blow up a refrigerator?"

"It doesn't explode," Mya told him.

"Then how will it save my life?" Coke asked.

"It won't save your life," Mya explained. "It will make your refrigerator look nice."

Coke shook his head and gave the magnet to Pep so she could add it to her collection.

"Just leave us alone, okay?" he said to Mya and Bones. "We don't need your help anymore."

Chapter 22

BREAKING AND ENTERING

"**W**hat's eating *you*?" Dr. McDonald asked as Coke climbed into the car with a scowl on his face.

"Nothin'."

"Didn't you kids find those mammoths to be fascinating?" their mother asked. "I got a lot of material for *Amazing but True*."

Coke and Pep grunted. Their parents glanced at each other and rolled their eyes.

Teenagers. Who can figure 'em out?

"Well, I think you're *really* going to like our next

stop," Mrs. McDonald said optimistically.

They had lunch at a Waco restaurant called Buzzard Billy's, and then drove a few miles to the south side of town, the industrial district of Waco. Dr. McDonald pulled up to a huge, boxy building with an empty parking lot. A sign on the side of the building said . . .

MARS
chocolate
north america

Coke and Pep were instantly intrigued. Chocolate cures all ills.

"Mars?" Pep asked. "You mean like the candy bars?"

"The company makes Skittles, Starburst, Milky Way, and Snickers here," her mother replied, leafing through her guidebook. "In fact, it says that if you're eating a Snickers bar anywhere in North America, there's a ninety-six percent chance that it was made right here at this factory."

"Wow," Coke said. "This is gonna be cool!"

"Why do you think the parking lot is empty?" asked Dr. McDonald.

"I guess we're a little early for the tour," Pep said.

As they stepped out of the car, they could smell the chocolate—a *wonderful* smell.

Coke pulled on the front door of the building, but it was locked. A small sign stated the obvious—CLOSED.

"Closed?!" Mrs. McDonald took out her cell phone and dialed the number in her guidebook. After wading through several frustrating layers of computerized options, she finally punched in *0* and got a human being at the other end of the line.

"We're standing at the front door of your factory, and it's locked," she explained politely. "We're here to take the two o'clock tour."

"I'm terribly sorry, ma'am," said the voice at the other end of the line, *"but we don't have a tour."*

"It says on the internet that you have a guided tour every day of the week at ten, noon, two, and four o'clock," Mrs. McDonald said, her voice rising.

"Calm down, Bridge," said Dr. McDonald.

"That must be a mistake, ma'am," said the voice. *"There is no tour. And the factory is closed today, anyway."*

Now she was mad.

"What do you mean, it's *closed*?" Mrs. McDonald shouted. "We drove all the way across the country to come here. My kids were so excited. They've been sitting in the car for five hours."

"We have not, Mom," Pep whispered.

"Shhhhhh!"

"I'm sorry, ma'am—"

"Do you have any idea who I am?" Mrs. McDonald shouted into the phone.

"No ma'am, I don't."

"I am the creator of *Amazing but True*, one of the most popular reference sites on the web. *ABT* gets over a million hits each month. My readers are not going to be happy when I tell them about this. You don't want a boycott on your hands."

"Bridge, let it go," Dr. McDonald said.

"I'm sure your website is very influential," the voice on the phone said, *"but we simply don't offer a tour. We never did."*

"Let me ask you a question," Mrs. McDonald said, trying to remain calm. "What if the president of the United States came here today and asked for a tour of the factory? Do you think you might find a way to open up and show him around?"

"I suppose we would, yes," the voice said.

"Well, I have news for you. The president *isn't* gonna show up today. But we did. How about you give us the tour you would have given the president?"

"I'm sorry, ma'am. I wish I could help you."

"Well, that's the last pack of M&M's *I'll* ever buy," Mrs. McDonald said indignantly as she hung up. "Come on, gang, let's blow this pop stand."

Disappointed, the family climbed into the Ferrari. But as Dr. McDonald turned the key in the ignition, he got a gleam in his eye. He revved the engine, and instead of driving out of the parking lot, he drove slowly around to the back of the factory.

"Ben, where are you going?" asked Mrs. McDonald.

"If they won't give us a tour," he replied, "maybe we can take our *own* tour."

"Dad, you are such an outlaw!" Coke said with admiration. "It must be the Ferrari."

"I don't have a good feeling about this," Pep said.

The rear of the Mars factory had multiple entrances. Dr. McDonald drove slowly, looking for a door or window that might be open. He stopped the car and got out.

"Follow me," he said.

"This is insanity!" Mrs. McDonald complained, but she got out of the car anyway. "I'm sure they have security cameras, alarm systems, armed guards—"

"Chill, Bridge," Dr. McDonald said. "This is one of those unexpected pleasures of cross-country travel that you're always talking about."

"No, it's not," she replied. "It's breaking and entering."

"We're not going to break anything," Dr. McDonald said, looking around for security cameras, alarm systems, or armed guards. "We're just going to enter. Look, this window isn't locked."

"It's probably a felony," Mrs. McDonald fretted. "Or a misdemeanor. Or one of those crimes that criminals always commit."

"I can fit through that window," Coke said, climbing up to push it all the way open.

"Good job, son!" Dr. McDonald said.

Coke squeezed through the opening and landed on his feet inside the building. No alarms went off. He reached his hand out the window to pull his sister up.

"We're going to get caught," Pep said. "I don't want to go to jail."

"You're a minor," her father told her. "You *can't* go to jail."

"No, they'll put *you two* in jail for bad parenting," Pep said, "and then they'll put Coke and me in an orphanage, or one of those homes for juvenile delinquents."

"Oh, don't be such a baby," Dr. McDonald said, hoisting her up. "This is going to be fun. Believe me, if this place was open today, you wouldn't remember the experience. But because we're sneaking in, you'll remember it for the rest of your life."

Pep reluctantly squeezed through the window, and Coke helped her inside.

"You're next, Bridge," Dr. McDonald said.

"Oh, no. Not me," she replied. "I'm staying out here. Somebody's going to have to post bail for you three."

"Suit yourself," Dr. McDonald said, hoisting himself up.

Unfortunately, Dr. McDonald was more than a few pounds heavier than either of the twins. He could fit his head and shoulders through the narrow window, but his stomach stubbornly refused to squeeze through.

"!@#$%," he cursed. "Pardon my French."

"Dad, you need to go on a diet," Coke teased.

"All right," Dr. McDonald said, pulling himself back outside. "You kids go ahead. Mom and I will wait in the car."

"Promise you'll visit us when we're in juvie," Pep said.

"You're *not* going to juvie," insisted Dr. McDonald. "Someday, you'll appreciate how cool your parents were."

Coke took his sister by the hand and led her out of the little room, which was filled with janitorial supplies. A short hallway led to the main floor of the factory. The place was enormous, and it was filled with gigantic machines and aluminum vats. With no other people around and all the machines idle, it was eerily quiet.

"This place is *cool*," Coke marveled. "Can you imagine how many candy bars they can make from the chocolate in just one of those vats?"

The twins walked around hesitantly, expecting an alarm to sound at any moment. When it didn't, they grew bolder, examining the equipment and venturing farther inside the factory. They had just about lowered their guard entirely when they heard a noise behind them. Coke and Pep spun around to see a shadowy figure standing about fifteen yards away.

"I knew you wouldn't be able to resist breaking in here," he said, stepping into the light. It was a familiar voice.

"Dr. Warsaw!" the twins shouted simultaneously.

Chapter 23

DEATH BY CHOCOLATE

Coke and Pep's first reaction was to make a run for it. They *should have* made a run for it. But there was something that stopped them. The figure looked just like Dr. Warsaw, but something was slightly different. It was hard to put a finger on it.

"Are you . . . Dr. Warsaw's clone?" Pep asked, trembling.

"In a way, yes," the man said in a voice that sounded vaguely like the voice on a car navigation system. He took a step forward. "I could be his twin. I look more like Dr. Warsaw than you two look alike. I'm a perfect clone, you might say. But I'm not a clone in the biological sense of the word. You see, I'm a robot."

It took a moment for *that* to sink in.

"You *gotta* be kidding me," Coke said.

"Under my metal surface is a set of very complicated, sophisticated electronics," the robot said. "Twelve miles of wiring. Thousands of microprocessors. I possess all the information Dr. Warsaw does, and much more. And I know everything there is to know about you."

"It's a trick," Coke said. "You're no robot."

"Go ahead, Coke, touch me. I won't bite."

Coke stepped forward and reached out to touch the robot's hand. It was hard, not fleshy. It felt metallic. Coke made a mental note not to punch the robot. It would only break his own hand.

"Cold, isn't it?" the robot said.

"You're bluffing," Pep said. "You don't know about us. When is our birthday?"

"June twenty-fifth," the robot replied instantly. "Your home is in Point Reyes Station, California. You attend West Marin Middle School. Or you *did*, until it burned down under mysterious circumstances on the last day of school. And you each have a small birthmark on your right foot."

Pep gasped.

Coke peered into the robot's eyes. There was no way to tell it wasn't a human.

"You called me on the phone in our hotel room the other night," Coke said, "and you delivered that cipher through our car radio, didn't you?"

"Guilty as charged."

"What do the ciphers mean?" Pep asked. "Llano Estacado, a piece of the Blarney Stone, Hub City. What ties them together?"

"I'm just the messenger," replied the robot, "and you ask too many questions."

"Well, maybe you can answer *this* one," Coke said. "What are you doing here?"

The robot wheeled around on its heel slowly, gesturing in an almost human but slightly jerky fashion.

"Factories are special places," it said. "They're filled with robots, much like me. In fact, I was built right here. And *you* will die here."

"Ha!" Coke said. "You could never catch us. What prevents us from running away from you right now?"

"*This* does," the robot said.

At that instant, its hands telescoped out from its arms, like two antennas.

"Run, Pep!" Coke shouted, but it was too late. Each robot hand wrapped around a twin's neck in a tight grip, leaving no doubt that the grip could be tightened further, crushing their necks. Coke tried unsuccessfully to reach for the cell phone in his back pocket. Pep let out a shriek.

"Scream all you want," the robot said as it dragged them across the floor. "Besides you two, there's only one other human in the building."

At that, another figure stepped out from the shadows.

"Mrs. Higgins!" Pep shouted when she saw her.

"That's right," Mrs. Higgins said, taking a few steps closer. "I'm with *him* now. And we're in *love*."

"What?!" Pep said. "You told us you were in love with Dr. Warsaw."

"I was," Mrs. Higgins replied. "But Herman never returned my love. I'm not sure he's capable of loving *anyone*. And if I can't have him, I can have the next best thing. Isn't that right, honey?"

"That's right, dear," the robot said, and then it leaned over to kiss Mrs. Higgins.

"That's just sick!" Coke said. "You just kissed a robot."

"Who are you to judge our love?" Mrs. Higgins asked. "Soon you'll be dead, anyway."

"Sad but true," the robot said.

"Dad! Mom! Help!" Coke choked.

"Ha-ha!" Mrs. Higgins cackled. "I love to watch you

work, darling. You're even more cold-hearted than Herman was."

"Yes, Dr. Warsaw is distressed that he no longer possesses the ruthlessness necessary to kill you personally," said the robot. "Fortunately, he spent years designing me—an almost perfect copy of himself, minus the burden of a conscience or feelings of remorse. The good doctor affectionately calls me . . . Doominator."

Doominator stopped in front of a room-sized machine consisting of an endless series of wheels, gears, belts, lights, compartments, and switches. There was a one-word sign in front of it—SNICKERS.

"You're insane!" Pep shouted.

"Insane?" Doominator said. "The definition, according to my built-in dictionary, is 'of, pertaining to, or characteristic of a person who is mentally deranged.' No, I do not believe that I can be insane, as I am not—technically—a person."

With that, Doominator lifted Coke and Pep up by their necks and threw them roughly into two large metal boxes that were attached to a conveyor belt. Bars slammed down over the twins to prevent them from escaping.

"Do you like chocolate?" Doominator asked.

"Are you going to . . . drown us in it?" Pep asked,

holding back her sobs.

"Oh, no, that would be too easy," said Doominator as it flipped a switch. The machine lurched into motion. "This is a candy-wrapping machine."

"You're going to become rap stars!" cackled Mrs. Higgins. "I'm lovin' it!"

"Help!" Pep screamed. "I don't want to get wrapped!"

Peering through the bars, Pep could see a part of the machine with hundreds of unwrapped Snickers bars that were being fed into another part of the machine and other Snickers bars coming out the opposite end all wrapped up.

"You're going to be part of a long, proud tradition," Doominator shouted over the loud machinery. "Snickers was introduced way back in 1930. It was named after a horse that the Mars family owned on their Tennessee farm. Fifteen million Snickers bars are produced every day. And now, some of them will have a little Coke and Pepsi inside each one."

"You're going to . . . cut us up?" Coke asked.

"Of course not," Doominator said. "I share Dr. Warsaw's distaste for blood. We have *other* robots to do that. And then a third robot comes in afterward and cleans up the mess. That's the beauty of robotic technology. Division of labor. We hardly need any humans

anymore. Except for you, of course, dear."

"Apology accepted, my darling," said Mrs. Higgins.

The machinery was moving and whirring. Coke and Pep struggled to break out of their metal boxes. It was useless.

"Let us *out*!" Pep screamed.

"That's cute," Doominator said. "But think of the joy you will bring to little children when they bite into that delicious nougat topped with caramel, peanuts, milk chocolate, and tiny chunks of Coke and Pepsi."

"That's gross!" Pep screamed.

"I'd love to stand here and debate this with you," Doominator said, "but Mrs. Higgins and I have a busy day. You're not the only geniuses that need to be eliminated, you know."

"No! We'll do anything you want!" Coke shouted. "Don't leave!"

"I think it was Shakespeare who said 'Parting is such sweet sorrow,'" said Doominator. "But perhaps you'll be my chocolate treat tomorrow. Ha-ha-ha!"

Doominator and Mrs. Higgins walked away holding hands, leaving the twins to struggle for their lives inside their steel cages.

Clearly, this was the end. There was no escape. They would be sliced, diced, molded, injected, wrapped, boxed, and distributed in Snickers bars. Their metal cages lurched forward and into the huge candy-wrapping machine.

"I love you, Coke!" Pep shouted.

"I love you too!"

"What? Did you just say you love me?"

Even in her perilous situation, Pep was stunned. Coke had never uttered those words before. He and she had fought like cats and dogs over the years. But in the past few weeks alone, they had been through so many hardships, and they had always stuck together. Tears flowed down her cheeks.

"Do something!" Pep shouted desperately as they moved closer to the innards of the machine.

"Like what?" Coke shouted back. "How about *you* come up with a brilliant idea for a change?"

But in fact, at that moment, Coke himself came up with a brilliant idea.

"Wait! I've got something!" he shouted.

"What? What is it?"

"The backscratcher!" Coke yelled. "The telescoping backscratcher that Mya and Bones gave us! I keep it inside my pants leg!"

"Why would you keep a backscratcher inside your pants leg?" Pep asked.

"Yeah, *do* complain!" Coke scolded her. "You never know when you might need to scratch your back."

He reached down to pull up the right leg of his jeans. The backscratcher was tucked inside his sock. He pulled it out and opened it up as far as it would go. Extended, it was eighteen inches long.

As their metal cages moved along the conveyor belt, Coke poked the backscratcher through the bars and tried to disrupt the gears and wheels on the right side. The machinery was within reach, but Coke had to be careful not to drop the backscratcher or let it get snapped in two.

They were now only a few feet away from the innards of the machine, where the unthinkable would happen. Sweat was pouring off Coke's forehead as he manipulated the backscratcher with his fingertips.

"Hurry!" Pep shouted.

And then, seconds before their cages would have dropped into the guts of the machine, Coke found a vulnerable spot. He poked the backscratcher into the blades of a small fan. The blades stopped, which sent a signal to the computer controlling the machine, and the whole thing ground to a halt.

Silence. Sweet silence. And then, a voice.

"Coke! Pepsi! Are you in there?"

"Yes!"

"In here!"

"Mom? Dad?"

But it wasn't their mother or father who had come to rescue them. The parents were still waiting patiently in the car. The gears of the wrapping machine were put into reverse and the cages were backed out until Coke and Pep could see who had come to save them.

"Bones! Mya!" Pep hollered. "What are *you* doing here?"

"You didn't think we gave up on you two, did you?" Mya asked as she opened the cage and helped Pep climb out of it.

"I did, actually," Coke said as Bones opened his cage. "But I'm glad I was wrong."

Chapter 24

KEEPING AUSTIN WEIRD

Except for a rip in Coke's T-shirt, the twins were fine. They told Mya and Bones everything they could remember about Doominator and Mrs. Higgins.

"Let's go!" Bones hollered to Mya. "Maybe we can catch them before they get too far."

Before following him, Mya put her hands on the twins' shoulders.

"We will watch out for you, *always*," she said. Then she hugged them both and ran after Bones.

Coke and Pep had no interest in hanging around to see the rest of the chocolate factory. They rushed back to the little storage room and climbed out the small window they had entered. Their parents were waiting in the car.

"So, did you have fun?" asked Dr. McDonald. "Was it exciting, having the run of the place?"

"*Exciting* is the perfect word for it, Dad," Coke replied.

"Not *again*!" Mrs. McDonald asked, poking her finger through the tear in Coke's shirt. "What happened *this* time?"

"It . . . uh . . . got caught on something," Coke said honestly. "I'm really sorry, Mom."

"I wish you'd be more careful," Mrs. McDonald said shaking her head. "I feel like you ruin a new T-shirt just about every day."

Afterward, they had dinner and checked into a Waco hotel called La Quinta Inn & Suites. It was still early, and the twins, in the privacy of their own room, had some time to talk things over.

"Do you think that robot is as dangerous to us as the real Dr. Warsaw?" Pep wondered as she brushed her teeth.

"It's *more* dangerous," Coke replied. "At least Dr. Warsaw felt guilty about what he was doing. That's probably why he had a nervous breakdown. Doominator has everything Dr. Warsaw has, except for a conscience. So the robot can kill a kid and feel no remorse."

"Do you think Mrs. Higgins really loves him?" Pep asked. "I mean, is it possible to fall in love with a robot? Or for a robot to fall in love with a person?"

"Beats me," her brother replied. "The two of them seem like they're meant for each other. They're both psychos."

❦

Go to Google Maps (http://maps.google.com).

Click Get Directions.

In the A box, type Waco TX.

In the B box, type Austin TX.

Click Get Directions.

From Waco to Austin is a straight shot south about a hundred miles down I-35. In the morning, Dr. McDonald let the Ferrari unwind and they made the trip in an hour and a half.

As soon as they arrived in Austin, it was obvious that this was not your typical central Texas town. Besides its fame as the Live Music Capital of the World, Austin is also famous simply for being a weird place and proud of it. In fact, bumper stickers and signs around town say KEEP AUSTIN WEIRD.

From the giant fork outside the Hyde Park Bar & Grill to the mural of a frog saying HI, HOW ARE YOU, the town has a refreshing oddball character to it. Nothing says that more than the Museum of the Weird on East Sixth Street. That's exactly where Mrs. McDonald

wanted to go to gather material for *Amazing but True*.

People who are fascinated by UFOs, ghosts, sideshow freaks, and zombies feel right at home in this place. It's filled with displays of shrunken heads, Fiji

mermaids, Bigfoot footprints, live reptiles, wax vampires, mummies, and strange animals like a hairy fish and a two-headed cow. There's a photo of a football team with six-fingered players.

"This place creeps me out," Pep said as she gazed at an exhibit about Ballyhoo Betty, a professional fire-eater who pulls nails out of her nose. But Pep made it a point to look at every photo on the wall and peer into every display case.

Mrs. McDonald took a few pictures and jotted down some notes, but the Museum of the Weird was a little too weird even for her. And Dr. McDonald looked down his nose at the whole operation.

"They call *this* a museum?" he said with a snort. "That's ridiculous. Your mother and I will meet you outside."

After their parents left, the twins continued looking at the displays and giggling at the outrageousness of it all.

On a table near the shrunken head display was a button that looked like a doorbell. On a piece of paper next to it, somebody had written in childish handwriting. . . .

PUSH THIS BUTTON FOR A SURPRISE

Coke, intrigued, pushed the button. A voice came

out of a little speaker. . . .

"*7-14-12-4-14-5-19-7-4-2-17-8-2-10-4-19-12-0-18-19-4-17.*"

"It must be busted," Coke said. He pushed the button again.

"*7-14-12-4-14-5-19-7-4-2-17-8-2-10-4-19-12-0-18-19-4-17.*"

"I don't think it's busted," Pep said. "I think it's a cipher."

"Oh no, not another one," Coke groaned. "Not *numbers*!"

"Relax," his sister told him. "We can do this."

"Maybe *you* can do it," Coke replied. "I'm useless."

"Well, then memorize the numbers, at least," Pep instructed him.

"I already did."

That was the last thing either of them would do at the Museum of the Weird. At that moment, everything went black. Heavy blankets were thrown over the twins' heads, and then wrapped up tightly. It all happened so fast, there was no time to react. They were grabbed roughly from behind, picked up, and carried out the back exit.

Chapter 25

GOING FOR A RIDE

oke felt himself being carried down a flight of stairs, out a door, around a corner, and then up another flight of stairs.

"Help!" he could hear his sister shouting. But her voice was muffled, as she, too, was wrapped tightly inside a heavy blanket.

Finally, both twins were unwrapped so they could see their kidnappers.

"Bowler dudes!" Pep shouted. "Not *again*!"

"At your service," said the bowler dude with the mustache.

"At your service," repeated the clean-shaven bowler dude.

"I said that already."

"And I said it again."

"Shut up."

"*You* shut up."

Aside from the arguing bowler dudes, it was an empty room. There were no windows, and there was just one door. One way out, and the bowler dudes were blocking it.

"What are you going to do to us *now*?" Coke asked defiantly.

"You'll find out," the clean-shaven bowler dude said, snickering. With that, both bowler dudes left the room, locking the door behind them.

Pep let out the best scream she could muster, but the room was soundproof, of course. Coke looked around for an escape route. There were no vents in the floor, walls, or ceiling. He reached for the cell phone in his back pocket. It was gone. Pep's had been taken away too.

When a half hour had passed and the twins hadn't come out of the Museum of the Weird, their parents went inside to get them. Coke and Pep, of course,

were no longer there.

"Have you seen two kids?" Dr. McDonald asked the lady behind the ticket booth. "A boy and a girl? Twins? They're thirteen."

"Yeah, I think I saw them in here earlier," the lady replied. "Maybe fifteen minutes ago. They must have left."

Dr. and Mrs. McDonald rushed outside and looked up and down the busy street. There were a lot of kids milling around. But not *their* kids.

Reader, as a young person, you can't imagine the feeling that comes over parents when they're out in a public place and their children suddenly are not where they expect them to be. In a matter of seconds, the parents will go from calm and relaxed to believing they will never see their children again.

Dr. McDonald dialed the cell phone numbers for Coke and Pep. No answer. Now the McDonalds were getting frantic. The next call was to the police.

The twins were locked in a room just a few blocks away, but there was no way of knowing that. There was nothing for *them* to do either. Hours passed. At some point, the door flew open and one of the bowler dudes slid in a tray with two burritos on it. Then the door slammed shut again. Other than that, there was no communication. The twins lost track of time.

"Why do you think they're holding us here?" Pep asked her brother. "If they wanted to do something to us, they could have done it already."

"It's almost like they're waiting for something," Coke replied.

They were.

The nice detective at the police station helped Mrs. McDonald file a missing persons report. The police would comb the city looking for the twins, she explained calmly. Kids get reported missing all the time. More often than not, they stray a hundred yards from their parents or wander off in search of ice cream. On the very rare occasion, a kid is kidnapped. But all threats must be taken seriously.

Just before dusk, the door abruptly opened again and both of the bowler dudes came into the room. It was almost a relief for the kids to see human beings, even if it had to be *those* human beings. The mustachioed one was carrying two rags and some thick rope. He proceeded to tie the twins' hands behind their backs and blindfold them.

"Get your paws off of me!" Coke shouted, trying

to karate-kick the clean-shaven bowler dude. He knocked the bowler hat off the dude's head but didn't inflict any damage.

The big man was not amused. He picked up Coke and hoisted him over his shoulder. His brother did the same to Pep.

"Where are you taking us?" she demanded. "Leave us alone!"

"You're going for a ride," the clean-shaven bowler dude said. "Kids like rides, don't you?"

The twins couldn't see where they were being taken, but they could tell they were carried downstairs and thrown roughly into a van. The ride was short, less than five minutes. They couldn't have traveled even a mile. Coke spent the time trying to free his hands behind his back, but the rope was expertly tied.

The van came to a stop. The doors opened. The bowler dudes weren't talking. Coke and Pep felt themselves being picked up and carried a short distance. It was quieter here. The sounds of the city were more distant.

They felt themselves being lowered carefully onto something. It was wobbly, not a solid surface. There was the sound of water underneath.

"I think we're in a boat," Coke said. "A little boat."

"And I'd advise you not to try anything stupid, like jumping out of it," one of the bowler dudes said. "It's really hard to swim with your hands tied behind your back."

"Gee, thanks for the advice," Coke replied sarcastically. "You're a big help. Do you have any other pearls of wisdom for us?"

"Yeah, have fun!" shouted one of the bowler dudes.

With that, he gave the rowboat a shove with his foot, pushing it out onto the Colorado River.

When I say Colorado River, you're probably thinking of white-water rafting through the Grand Canyon. It certainly would be a terrifying experience to go through rapids on a rowboat, blindfolded, with your hands tied behind your back.

But that's a *different* Colorado River. The Colorado around Austin is a slow-moving river, with dams that created man-made lakes within the city limits. The rowboat floated almost peacefully away from the shore.

"Where are we?" Pep asked.

"On a lake or a river," Coke replied. "Probably a river. I feel movement."

He struggled to free his hands from the ropes. It was hot, and he was sweating. Coke was careful not to rock the boat. Capsizing it could be catastrophic.

"What if we're going to go over a waterfall?" Pep asked, sudden panic in her voice. "What if we're going to go over Niagara Falls!"

"This is *Texas*, you dope," her brother replied. "Here, let's turn around so we're back-to-back. Then you can try to loosen my rope, and I can try to loosen yours."

Very carefully, the twins maneuvered around in the little rowboat until they were facing in opposite directions. Pep's fingers were slightly smaller than her brother's, which made it easier for her to pick at the knot.

Working together, they were making progress. If they could loosen their hands, they could get the blindfolds off their faces. Then they'd be free.

"What's that squeaking noise?" Pep asked as she worked at the rope.

"It sounds like birds," her brother replied.

"They're getting closer," Pep said, "and I think something just dripped on my head. Ewww, what is that *smell*?"

"Forget the smell," Coke replied excitedly. "I'm almost free!"

The last knot came loose. Coke pulled the rope off his hands and ripped the blindfold from his face. Instantly, he saw what was making the noise and the smell.

"Bats!" he shouted.

Yes, bats. Not the kind you use to hit a baseball. I'm talking about furry, flying mammals with webbed wings. *Those* kinds of bats.

It just so happens that the largest urban bat colony in North America lives under the Congress Avenue Bridge in Austin, Texas. Every day around sunset, more than a million Mexican free-tailed bats emerge from the underside of the bridge and go out for dinner at the same time.

With her brother's help, Pep ripped the blindfold off her face, but maybe she shouldn't have. A three-and-a-half-inch gray bat was flying directly toward her head, only to veer away at the last instant.

"Eeeeeeeeeeeeeek!" Pep screamed, ducking and covering her face. "They're *everywhere*!"

Indeed they were. The swarm of bats coming from the bottom of the bridge was like a dark cloud swirling around the little boat. Mexican free-tailed bats can fly as fast as sixty miles per hour, diving, twisting, screeching, and crapping the whole time. *Anyone* would be terrified to be in the middle of them.

"Stay still!" Coke shouted over the screeching.

"Are you crazy?" Pep shrieked back. "Bats suck blood! They have rabies! I'm covered in bat poop!"

"They aren't aggressive!" Coke insisted. "Bats don't

care about people! They eat insects!"

Well, he was right about *that*. A bat's diet consists of moths, beetles, dragonflies, wasps, and ants. They can consume up to one-half of their body weight in insects each night.

"But there are *millions* of them!" Pep shrieked, waving her arms around frantically. "And they're blind! They're blind as bats!"

"Be calm! Close your eyes!" Coke advised. "They use echolocation for navigation and detecting prey! They won't touch you!"

He was right about that too. Bats "see" with their ears. They emit noises and listen to the echoes to sense objects around them. That's how they avoid flying into things, such as people who happen to be sitting in boats under bridges.

"Screw that!" Pep screamed. "I'm outta here!"

With that, she hurled herself off the side of the boat.

"Come to think of it, that's not a bad idea," Coke said, just before diving into the river himself.

Their heads popped out of the water at the same time. The swarm of bats was even thicker now. They almost blocked out the sky.

"Get underwater!" Pep shouted.

Both twins filled their lungs with air and submerged

for as long as they could hold their breath. When Coke finally came up for air, the bats were still swarming all over. He gulped some air and swam under the rowboat, pushing it from the bottom to turn it upside down and create a little shelter over his head. Pep surfaced and ducked under the boat too.

After what seemed like forever—but was actually just a few minutes—the last of the bats had flown out from under the bridge. The air was suddenly still. It was over. It would be a while until all those bats returned from dinner.

Together, exhausted, the twins swam toward the riverbank. When they made it to the edge, two hands reached down to pull them up on the shore.

It was their parents.

"You two are *so* grounded!" their father shouted.

Chapter 26

ANOTHER CLUE

A s soon as Coke and Pep got out of the water, their parents were all over them, like bats under a bridge.

"Where have you two *been* all day?"

"We told you to meet us outside the *museum*!"

"Why were you in the *river*?"

"What were you *thinking*?"

"You had us worried *sick*!"

"We were scared to *death*!"

"We filed a *police report*!"

Pep looked to her brother, as usual, to do the talking.

"Okay, here's what happened," Coke tried to explain. "We were kidnapped from the museum by these guys in bowler hats. They locked us in a room all afternoon. Then they tied us up and brought us out to the river. They put us in a boat and the bats came out and—"

"Don't give me that, mister!" Dr. McDonald shouted. "We've heard enough of your wild stories!"

The parents were even angrier when they found out the twins no longer had their cell phones. Not a word was spoken in the car on the way to the Econo Lodge Arboretum in North Austin. Coke and Pep knew that any excuse they could come up with wouldn't fly with their parents.

"You are *not* to leave this room tonight," Dr. McDonald said coldly after they had checked into the hotel. "You are *not* to turn on the TV. You are *not* to take anything out of the minibar. Do you understand me?"

"Yeah," both twins replied glumly.

"In case of emergency—and there *better not* be an emergency—your father and I will be listening to music at Antone's on Fifth Street," said Mrs. McDonald. "You two can sit here and think about what you did."

After their parents left, Coke and Pep took showers and changed into dry clothes. They tried reading for a while, but it was hard to focus after what they had been through.

"Want to watch TV?" Coke asked.

"Mom and Dad told us we weren't allowed to watch TV."

"How are they gonna know?"

"They'll know," Pep said. "There's probably a chip in the TV that records what we watch."

"You're paranoid."

There was nothing else to do. A thought popped into Pep's head. They had received a new cipher when they were at the Museum of the Weird. She didn't remember it, but her brother would. She got out her notepad and had him write the cipher down:

7-14-12-4-14-5-19-7-4-2-17-8-2-10-4-19-12-0-18-19-4-17

Coke looked at the numbers and shook his head. It was impossible.

"Think of it this way," Pep said. "Each number probably stands for a letter. We just have to break it down and figure out which one."

Pep wrote out the alphabet, and then put the numbers *1* through *26* under the letters.

A B C D E F G H I J K L M N O P Q R S T U V W X Y Z
1 2 3 4 5 6 7 8 9 10 11 12 13 14 15 16 17 18 19 20 21 22 23 24 25 26

"This would be the simplest solution," she continued. "The number *7* is under *G*, so *7* probably means *G*. The number *14* is under *N*, so the second letter is *N*."

"There aren't many words that start with *GN*," Coke noted. "Gnat, gnome . . ."

Pep went on, and decoded the first ten letters. It spelled *GNLDNESGDB*.

"I made a mistake somewhere," she said, looking up. "This doesn't make any sense."

"Maybe you put the wrong numbers under the letters," her brother suggested.

Pep looked at the letters and numbers for a few minutes, and then crossed out everything she had written. Below, she wrote the alphabet out again, this time starting with a zero under the letter *A*, number *1* under the letter *B*, number *2* under the letter *C*, and so on.

A	B	C	D	E	F	G	H	I	J	K	L	M	N	O	P	Q	R	S	T	U	V	W	X	Y	Z
0	1	2	3	4	5	6	7	8	9	10	11	12	13	14	15	16	17	18	19	20	21	22	23	24	25

"So now the *7* is under the letter *H*," Pep said. "So *7* must mean *H*. And *14* is under the letter *O*, so *14* must mean *O*. The first two letters are *H-O*."

"*M* is above *12*, so *12* means *M*," Coke said. "*E* is above *4*, so *4* means *E*."

"The first four letters are *H-O-M-E*," Pep said,

writing them out excitedly.

They continued like that, matching up the numbers with the letters directly above them. Soon they had the whole message:

HOMEOFTHECRICKETMASTER

"Home of the cricket master!" Pep exclaimed. "That's what it means! But what's a cricket master?"

"There used to be a video game called Cricket Master," Coke recalled, "I think I played it once at somebody's birthday party."

Pep went to the other side of the room to get her mother's laptop computer. They were told that they weren't allowed to turn on the TV. Nobody said they couldn't use the computer.

She Googled "Cricket Master." Naturally, twenty-seven *million* results came up. A lot of them concerned the video game Coke had mentioned. There was also a British cricket player named Jack Hobbs, who was known as "the Master." But none of the results seemed to mean anything important.

"We struck out *again*," Pep said. "'Cricket master' has nothing to do with *anything*."

"*Nothing* has anything to do with anything!" Coke said in frustration. "None of these clues connect with any of the other clues."

Nevertheless, Pep added the new one to her list. . . .

1. I WILL MEET YOU IN LLANO ESTACADO
2. A PIECE OF THE BLARNEY STONE
3. HUB CITY
4. TEXAS RANGER
5. HOME OF THE CRICKET MASTER

Go to Google Maps
(http://maps.google.com).

Click Get Directions.

In the A box, type
Austin TX.

In the B box, type
San Antonio TX.

Click Get Directions.

235

Chapter 27

MAJORITY RULES

When Dr. and Mrs. McDonald got back to the hotel later that night, they were in a much better frame of mind. They even brought back a souvenir—a KEEP AUSTIN WEIRD refrigerator magnet. But Coke and Pep were asleep. Escaping from a swarm of bats does tend to sap your energy.

In the morning, the family set out for San Antonio, which is eighty miles south of Austin on I-35. The angry feelings of the night before were gone, or at least pushed below the surface for the time being.

"What's in San Antonio?" Pep asked, not sure she wanted to know the answer.

"The Alamo, of *course*," her father replied.

"Isn't that a rental car place?" Coke asked. "Why would we want to go *there*?"

Coke knew what the Alamo was. He just felt like giving his dad a hard time.

"The Alamo is *not* a rental car place!" his exasperated father replied. "It's an eighteenth-century mission church where the pivotal battle in the fight for the independence of Texas took place. Don't they teach you kids *anything* in school?"

"Texas is independent?" Pep asked.

Mrs. McDonald laughed. The Ferrari almost drove off the road.

"Look," Dr. McDonald said, "in the early 1800s, Texas belonged to Mexico. The Texans fought a war for independence in 1836. There was a thirteen-day siege, and a few hundred Texans were badly outnumbered at the Alamo. Finally, fifteen hundred Mexican troops launched an assault and wiped them out. Guys like James Bowie, Davy Crockett, and William Travis died. And ever since that day, the Alamo has symbolized courage and sacrifice for the cause of liberty. You've heard the phrase 'Remember the Alamo.' That was Sam Houston's battle cry when he defeated General Santa Anna a few weeks later. Texas became an independent republic and then joined the United States as the twenty-eighth state. Won't it be

interesting to go to the Alamo and see where this all happened?"

"I guess," the twins mumbled, which, translated into the language of Teenager, means "No."

"*Everybody* goes to the Alamo, Ben," Mrs. McDonald said. "Do you want to be just another sheep following the herd?"

Dr. McDonald was getting progressively more steamed. Now he had to take guff from his wife too.

"Everybody goes to the Alamo because it's an important part of American history! It's a part of our democracy we all should know," he said, a little too loud.

"Actually," Mrs. McDonald said, "there's another place I'd like to go that's right near San Antonio."

"Where?"

"You're just going to laugh."

"We won't laugh, Mom," promised Pep.

"The Toilet Seat Art Museum," she said.

Everybody laughed.

"That's a joke, right, Bridge?" asked Dr. McDonald.

"No, it's not."

"You gotta be kidding me," Coke said. "There's a museum devoted to toilet seats?"

"It's not devoted to toilet seats," Mrs. McDonald replied. "It's devoted to toilet seat *art*."

Dr. McDonald had just about reached his limit.

"Another tourist trap?" he said. "Bridge, just because some guy collected a bunch of junk in his garage and calls it a museum doesn't mean we have to go *look* at it."

"Oh, come on, Ben," Mrs. McDonald said. "It will be great for *Amazing but True.*"

"How about we take a vote on it?" Coke suggested. "That's the way democracy works, right? What do you vote for, Dad, the Alamo or the toilet seat place?"

"The Alamo."

"How about you, Mom?"

"The toilet seat art museum."

"What about you, Pep?"

"The toilet seat art museum."

"I vote for the toilet museum too," Coke said. "That's three to one. Majority rules. *Woo-hoo!* We're going to look at toilet seats! Isn't democracy wonderful?"

Pep peeked at her father's face in the rearview mirror. It looked like he might have a seizure.

"Why can't we go to *both* places?" Pep suggested. "We can spend the morning at the toilet seat art museum and the afternoon at the Alamo. Everybody will be happy. Democracy is all about compromises, right?"

Dr. McDonald abruptly swerved the car and pulled off onto the shoulder of the highway. He took off his seat belt so he could turn around to address the whole family.

"Look," he said, trying his best to remain calm. "I went along with the yo-yo museum and the Spam museum. I went to the mustard museum and the Waffle House museum. I even went with you to that stupid washing machine museum. But life is short. I'm *not* going to waste half a day looking at toilet seats. And that's *final*!"

"So much for your compromises," Coke mumbled to his sister.

"How about this idea, Dad?" Pep suggested. "You drop the three of us off at the toilet seat art museum and then you can go visit the Alamo on your own. We can meet up later."

Dr. McDonald thought it over. Part of him didn't like Pep's idea. They were a *family*. The whole idea of driving cross-country was to explore America *together*. If they were to split up and do separate things instead of working out their differences, it would be like Abraham Lincoln telling the Confederacy, "Okay, you guys can be your own country, and we'll be our own country."

On the other hand, the Civil War had been a bloody mess. He had to admit that Pep's idea *was* a simple solution to the problem.

"Okay," he agreed. "Just this one time."

The museum just happened to be in Alamo Heights, a few miles north of San Antonio. Dr. McDonald took exit 159B and drove down Broadway Street almost all the way to Barney Smith's Toilet Seat Art Museum, which is so famous that Google Maps has it labeled. Go ahead and look it up if you don't believe me.

Mrs. McDonald grabbed her camera and computer case so she could file a report for *Amazing but True*.

"Have fun looking at the toilet seats!" Dr. McDonald hollered out the window before roaring off to the Alamo, in downtown San Antonio.

In fact, they *did* have fun. Starting in the 1980s, a retired plumber named Barney Smith began painting and engraving toilet seats. By 2010 he had over a thousand of them, carefully mounted in his garage.

"This is *way* more interesting than the Alamo," Coke said as soon as they went inside.

He was only partly kidding. Barney Smith's Toilet Seat Art Museum was filled with paintings of dogs, Miss America, yellow jackets, and the map of Texas. Some of the seats depicted memories of Mr. Smith's life, like vacations, anniversaries, and his grandchildren. Some had a sporting theme—Super Bowls, Olympics—or world events such as the Holocaust or Desert Storm. Some of the seats were collages, with license plates, Scrabble tiles, or computer keyboards

glued to the surface. One seat had a piece of the Berlin Wall embedded in it.

The place was fascinating. Coke, Pep, and their mom could have spent the whole day there.

"May I use your bathroom?" Mrs. McDonald asked the lady wearing a Barney Smith's Toilet Seat Art Museum T-shirt. "For some reason, this place makes me need to go."

"I'm sorry," the lady said, "but we don't have a bathroom."

"You have a thousand toilet seats, but no bathroom?" said Mrs. McDonald. "It's kind of an emergency."

"Okay, okay," the lady said, pointing toward the back door of the house.

Mrs. McDonald handed Pep her computer case to hold. While she was gone, the twins continued looking at the vast collection of toilet seat art. That's when they noticed this:

Pep stared at it for a minute. It didn't make any sense.

"Excuse me," she said to the lady, "but can you tell us what this means?"

The lady came closer to look at it.

"Hmmm," she said, "that's odd. I've never seen this toilet seat before. It wasn't here yesterday. Somebody must have left it here just this morning."

Coke and Pep looked at each other.

"It's a cipher," Pep said ominously.

"Oh no," he groaned. "Not another one. I give up."

"Ye of little faith," his sister said, reaching into her pocket for her little notepad and pen. "It's obviously not a transposition cipher. It's not a Caesar shift cipher. It's not an ogham or a pigpen. It's not a Vigènere."

"A *what*?" Coke asked.

"Forget it, it doesn't matter."

"It ends with a number," Coke noted. "And it's the only number there. What could *that* mean?"

"The *2* was probably just put in there to throw us off the track," Pep replied. "They do that sometimes, just to mess with your mind."

The twins looked at the cipher for a few minutes. And then, finally, it wasn't Pep who broke out into a big smile. It was her brother.

"Wait a minute!" Coke said excitedly. "You're over-thinking this. You're missing the forest for the trees."

"What do you mean?"

"It's backward, you dope!" he told her.

Coke traced his finger around the message on the toilet seat in reverse order . . .

2PMTOMORROWLANDOFJOY

"Land of joy!" Coke exclaimed, spectacularly proud of himself. It was the first cipher he had ever cracked on his own.

"You're right!" Pep said, punching her brother on the shoulder. "But what does 'land of joy' mean?"

"Google it," Coke said.

Pep took her mother's computer out of its case and typed "Land of Joy" into the search box.

"What does it say?" Coke asked, leaning over to see the screen.

"Land of Joy is a Buddhist retreat community in England," Pep said glumly.

Once again, they had received a cipher and solved it. And once again, it meant nothing. Disappointed, Pep scrawled the newest message at the bottom of her list:

1. I WILL MEET YOU IN LLANO ESTACADO
2. A PIECE OF THE BLARNEY STONE

3. HUB CITY
4. TEXAS RANGER
5. HOME OF THE CRICKET MASTER
6. 2 PM TOMORROW LAND OF JOY

What could any of that mean? What could those things possibly have in common?

You, dear reader, are about to find out.

Go to Google Maps (http://maps.google.com).

Click Get Directions.

In the A box, type San Antonio TX.

In the B box, type Lubbock TX.

Click Get Directions.

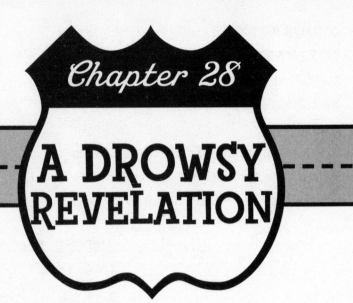

Chapter 28

A DROWSY REVELATION

The twins and their mom had to wait for a while, but eventually a candy-apple-red Ferrari roared into the driveway of Barney Smith's Toilet Seat Art Museum.

"You should have come with me to the Alamo," Dr. McDonald shouted out the window. "It was *amazing*."

"The toilet seat art was cool too, Dad," Pep told him.

The family had dinner at a pizza restaurant on San Antonio's River Walk and topped it off with ice cream sundaes. Their stomachs were full, and, after a quick stop on Cesar E. Chavez Boulevard, so was the gas tank. It was eight o'clock. Mrs. McDonald pulled out her guidebook to look up a nearby motel to spend the night.

"Y'know, I'm in a driving mood," Dr. McDonald announced. "Why don't you guys just relax and watch the scenery? When I see a decent motel, I'll pull in."

In the backseat, Coke scanned a magazine and Pep organized her growing collection of refrigerator magnets. She liked to look at them, and she had taken to carrying her favorites around in her pocket.

Maybe it was all the pizza and ice cream, but one by one Coke, Pep, and their mom dozed off. Dr. McDonald passed by several motels that had vacancy signs, but he didn't stop. It was so peaceful with the rest of the family sleeping. He didn't want to wake everybody up just so they could go back to sleep in a bed.

Besides, it was nice to have a little quiet for a change. It gave him time to think about his next book. The biography of President Hoover didn't look like it was going to work out. Neither did the book about Elvis Presley. He had to come up with another idea.

Soon summer and their cross-country trip would be over. It would be back to work teaching yawning freshmen about the causes of the Revolutionary War for the tenth year in a row. He wasn't looking forward to it. As the road unspooled before him, Dr. McDonald was lost in his thoughts. Dreams of seeing his name on the bestseller list danced in his head.

So he just kept driving west on I-10 from San Antonio. A detour at Comfort, Texas, forced him to take the smaller Route 87 North, which went through Brady, San Angelo, Big Spring, and Lamesa.

In this part of western Texas, there are no big cities, and some of the small towns didn't even have a stop sign. Just miles and miles of road. It was pitch-dark out and there were no streetlights. The only thing illuminating the pavement was the Ferrari's headlights. There wasn't another car around for miles.

"Don't mess with Texas, baby!" Dr. McDonald said to himself as the speedometer nosed past ninety miles per hour. The purr of the engine seemed to say *Thank you.* Signs warned of STRONG CROSSWINDS, but the Ferrari was designed to slice through the air like an arrow.

It wasn't until two o'clock in the morning that Dr. McDonald glanced at the odometer. He had driven nearly four hundred miles since leaving San Antonio. That's a *long* way to go without a bathroom break. Mrs. McDonald opened her eyes just in time to see a sign—LUBBOCK, 2 MILES.

"Ben, have you been driving all *night*?" she whispered, turning around to see that the twins were still asleep. "That's *crazy.*"

"I had a good time, actually," he replied. "No

yapping from the peanut gallery back there."

Mrs. McDonald opened her Texas guidebook.

"Lubbock is located in Llano Estacado," she read softly, *"a region of the southwestern United States that encompasses parts of eastern New Mexico and northwestern Texas. . . ."*

In the backseat, both twins suddenly opened their eyes.

"Did you say just say 'Estacado'?" Coke asked.

"Yes," his mother replied. "Llano Estacado."

The twins looked at each other with alarm. Llano Estacado. That was the first cipher!

"What else does it say in there, Mom?" Pep asked.

"Well, it says that Lubbock, Texas, is the economic, education, and health care hub of a multicounty region called the South Plain," she told them. "It's known as Hub City."

Coke and Pep's eyes opened wider.

"Lubbock is Hub City?" Coke asked.

"It also says that Lubbock was named after Thomas S. Lubbock," continued Mrs. McDonald, "who was a former Texas Ranger and Confederate officer—"

"He was a Texas Ranger?" Pep asked, slapping her head. "What *else* does it say?"

"Let's see," said Mrs. McDonald. "Lubbock was the birthplace of early rock and roll star Buddy Holly, who

created such memorable tunes as 'That'll Be the Day' and 'Peggy Sue' with the group he led, the Crickets."

"The Crickets?" shouted Coke.

"He was the Cricket Master!" Pep said.

"Hmm, this is interesting," Mrs. McDonald went on. "You'll never believe what they have on the campus of Texas Tech University in Lubbock."

"A piece of the Blarney Stone?" Coke and Pep asked simultaneously.

"How did *you* know?"

"It was a lucky guess," the twins replied.

"Does it say anything about Lubbock being a Land of Joy?" asked Pep.

"Land of Joy . . . Land of Joy . . . ," Mrs. McDonald mumbled as she paged through her guidebook. "No, but there *is* an amusement park in Lubbock."

"What's it called?" the twins asked.

"Joyland."

"Joyland!" Pep shouted. "That's Land of Joy!"

"We need to go there!" Coke shouted. "Tomorrow, at two o'clock."

"Why so specific?" asked Dr. McDonald.

"Please? Please? Please? Please?"

Dr. McDonald pulled off the road at the exit and spotted a sign for the Days Inn Lubbock South.

Chapter 29

JOYLAND

Coke couldn't sleep. He lay in bed thinking about his next twenty-four hours.

2 PM TOMORROW LAND OF JOY. Something was going to happen at Joyland Amusement Park. In all probability, he would have to confront Doominator, Dr. Warsaw's robot clone. It tried to kill him and Pep at the Mars factory, and it was sure to try again.

How do you kill a robot before it kills you? Robots don't bleed. They don't have a heart that can stop beating or a brain that can stop firing neurons. Doominator was more like a computer than like a human being.

But computers break down, Coke thought. Maybe he could disable it. Make it crash. Doominator said it had twelve miles of wiring inside it.

That gave Coke an idea.

Quietly, he got up from the bed, grabbed his wallet, tiptoed out of the room, and took the stairs down to the front desk of the hotel. Nobody was standing there in the middle of the night, but after a minute or so, a lady with tired eyes came out of the back room.

"May I help you?" she asked.

"Do you have a pair of wire cutters I could borrow?" Coke asked.

"Wire cutters? Hmmm, I don't know."

She was used to guests requesting toothbrushes or other toiletries they had forgotten to pack in their luggage. But nobody had ever asked for wire cutters before.

She rooted around in the drawers and a closet for a few minutes, and then, miraculously, she found what she was looking for.

"Do you mind my asking what you're planning to do with wire cutters?" she asked, before handing over the tool, which looked like a thick pair of scissors.

"Yeah, I'm planning to cut some wires," Coke replied. "How much do I owe you?"

"Well, I've been working here for ten years," the lady said, "and I've never had to use this thing once. Take it. Be careful. It's sharp."

Coke slipped two dollars onto the counter anyway and thanked the lady. He would be able to sleep now, knowing he had a weapon he could use against Doominator.

In the morning, their parents dragged—I mean *took*—the twins to the Buddy Holly Center in downtown Lubbock. It's a small museum honoring the rock and roll pioneer whose short career ended when he died in a 1959 plane crash. There was a film about Holly, lots of photos, clothes, and even his trademark glasses, which were recovered from the crash site in Iowa.

But the kids found it hard to pay much attention. Partly it was because Buddy Holly's music was from a different era. But mostly it was because they were nervous about what was going to happen in a few short hours.

Two o'clock. That's what the final cipher said—*2 PM TOMORROW LAND OF JOY.*

After lunch at the Cast Iron Grill, Dr. McDonald drove a couple of miles to Lubbock's Mackenzie State Park, where Joyland is located. As Dr. McDonald parked the

car, Pep was visibly nervous, even trembling.

"What's the plan?" she whispered to her brother. "We're walking into a trap. We don't even have any weapons this time."

Technically, that was true. When they confronted Evil Elvis at Graceland, they had a backpack stuffed with fireworks. Ultimately, that proved to be the undoing of Evil Elvis.

"Check this out," Coke said, pulling the wire cutters halfway out of his pocket. "One snip and Doominator is finished."

"Where'd you get *that*?" Pep asked.

"The front desk of the hotel," Coke replied. "I gave the lady two bucks for it."

"But how are you going to get to the wires?"

"Simple." I just have to break the skin and start cutting."

"Ugh, gross."

"Doominator's made of metal, remember?" Coke said. "It's not like I'll be cutting into flesh and bone. It can't feel pain."

Pep didn't have a lot of confidence in her brother's plan. So many things could go wrong. Maybe, if we're lucky, she thought, Mya and Bones will be there as backup. She remembered the last thing Mya said to her at the chocolate factory—"We will watch out for you, *always*."

Even so, Pep wished she had a weapon, like a Frisbee grenade. She would be able to fling it at Doominator and take the robot out from a distance.

It was one thirty when the McDonalds paid their admission and walked through the Joyland entrance gate. Getting there early was good, both twins thought. They could keep an eye out for the bowler dudes, Mrs. Higgins, and, of course, a robot named Doominator that looked strikingly like Dr. Warsaw.

Joyland doesn't pretend to be in a class with Six Flags, Cedar Point, Disney World, or any of the other giant amusement parks. It's smaller, more intimate, sort of retro. The best part is, the lines are shorter. You spend more time on the rides than you do wait-ing to get on the rides.

It was Texas hot, close to a hundred degrees. Noz-zles were scattered around to spray mists of cold water on people. Dr. McDonald closed his eyes for a moment to take in the clatter of the roller coasters and the aroma of cotton candy and fried dough. It brought back memories of his boyhood.

The family stopped in front of a map of Joyland. Even though the park was small, there were more than thirty rides and attractions. Everyone agreed it would be best to get an overview by taking Skyride, a ski-lift-style dangling cable car ride that runs the length of the park and provides a panoramic view from above.

Each chair holds just three passengers, so Dr. and Mrs. McDonald got on first and instructed the twins to get on the next chair. That was fine with Coke and Pep. They had work to do. They hopped on the next chair, and it slowly climbed to treetop level.

Below, they could see all of Joyland—the old-time carousel, the bumper cars, the Santa Fe Chief train ride. The chairlift slowly soared past Dare Devil Drop, Galaxi Coaster, Paratrooper, and the other thrill rides. The water rides—Big Splash Water Slide and the Vortex Water Coaster—were up ahead.

Coke's and Pep's feet dangled from the chair, and it looked as though they could step on the little people walking below. Carefully, they scanned the grounds on both sides looking for Doominator.

Little did they know that Doominator was *above* them.

Ten minutes earlier, the nimble robot had climbed a ladder to the top of the Skyride and waited for Coke and Pep's chair to pass underneath the little platform it was perched on. When the chair did, the robot pounced.

"Looking for *me*?" it said as it dropped onto the seat between the twins and clamped a steely arm around each one's shoulders. "Don't scream, or I'll snap both your necks like a couple of toothpicks."

It wouldn't have mattered if they *had* screamed.

The sound of people screaming on the nearby roller coasters would have drowned them out.

"Ahhh—" Pep said before a cold, metallic hand covered her face.

"You kids were pretty lucky getting out of the Snickers machine in Waco," Doominator said. "This time you won't be so fortunate. I'm going to get rid of you two once and for all."

"Wh-what are you going to do to us?" Coke asked, petrified.

"Oh, nothing fancy," the robot replied. "When we get over some nice hard asphalt, I'm going to throw you out of here. Depending on which body part hits the ground first, you'll probably be dead upon impact."

"You'll never get away with this!" Pep said.

She looked urgently at her brother. Coke was struggling to get his hand into his pocket to pull out the wire cutters.

"It will look like an accident," Doominator said casually. "People will say a couple of foolish kids were horsing around on the chairlift and fell off. Happens every day."

"Coke, do something!" Pep shouted.

At last, her brother was able to get the wire cutters out of his pocket. He wrapped his fist around the tool and jammed it into Doominator's thigh as hard as he could.

There was just one problem. The wire cutter didn't pierce the "skin."

Doominator, a sly grin on its face, looked up at Coke. The robot roughly snatched the wire cutter out of the boy's hand.

"Are you *joking*, with this toy?" Doominator said. "My body is made of *iron*, sonny. You think you're going to hurt me with *that*? All you did was ruin my new pants."

Doominator flung the wire cutter away and grabbed Coke by the throat.

"Okay, now it's time for you to *die*," it said.

"I'm sorry I ruined your pants!" Coke pleaded as he wrestled with the robot. "Stop! Don't! Please! I'm begging you!"

Pep started hitting Doominator, but it was no use. If only she had a weapon, something, *anything* she could use. Pep reached into her pocket and pulled out the first thing she touched—a refrigerator magnet in the shape of Oklahoma. It slipped out of her hand and landed on Doominator's left cheek, where it stuck.

"What's that?" the robot asked, waving its arms in front of its face.

"Get another one, Pep!" Coke shouted. "Quick!"

Pep reached into her pocket and pulled out her refrigerator magnet that was shaped like Arkansas.

258

She put it on Doominator's other cheek. The robot appeared disoriented.

"Got any more?" Coke asked urgently.

Pep emptied her pockets of all the refrigerator magnets she had and stuck them on every exposed body part on Doominator she could find.

"I don't care about my pants," Doominator said. "I don't care about my pants. I don't care about my pants. I don't care about my pants. . . ."

"What's happening?" Pep asked.

"You know how they say you shouldn't use magnets around your computer?" Coke said. "Doominator's like a computer! The refrigerator magnets are damaging its internal hard drive! I think it's gonna crash!"

There was a strange look on Doominator's face. Its mouth opened and closed rapidly, like a set of fake chattering teeth. Its left eye was blinking out of sync with its right eye. Its ears were twitching. It appeared to be having a seizure.

"Rewriting the bits . . . drive is polarized . . . ," Doominator said, slurring its words. "Data . . . is . . . corrupted . . . circuit board is unreadable . . . must reformat . . ."

That was the last thing the robot said. A moment later, its body convulsed and slipped off the chairlift. Coke and Pep leaned over to watch it tumble down

and land with a splash in the Wild River Log Flume.

Doominator was, in a matter of speaking, dead.

The twins were about to look up, but at that moment they both noticed a man limp over to the edge of the log flume. He was dressed exactly like Doominator.

"It's Dr. Warsaw!" Pep shouted. "The *real* one!"

They watched as Dr. Warsaw pulled Doominator's body out of the water and threw it roughly on the ground. Then he started shouting at it.

"I *knew* you would fail again, you incompetent nincompoop!" Dr. Warsaw hollered at Doominator. "I knew you were going to fail at the chocolate factory, so I gave you a second chance to take care of them here. And you failed me *again*!"

The robot was unresponsive. Not only had its hard drive been demagnetized, but having been soaked in water, it was completely lifeless.

"I spent *millions* creating you in my image," Dr. Warsaw yelled, beating on the robot's chest with his fists. "You were supposed to do what I could not. And now this. Why do my underlings always fail me? Why? I hate you! I hate myself!"

Go to Google Maps (http://maps.google.com).

Click Get Directions.

In the A box, type Lubbock TX.

In the B box, type Roswell NM.

Click Get Directions.

To passersby, it looked like Dr. Warsaw was giving CPR to revive a drowning man. Somebody must have dialed 911, because in seconds an ambulance and a police car were on the scene. Dr. Warsaw argued with the cops until they finally threw him into the squad car. The twins watched as it drove away.

The Skyride was nearing the end of its journey over Joyland.

"I just realized something," Pep said. "That's the third person we killed this summer."

"That one doesn't count," Coke replied. "It was a

robot. You can't kill a robot. And besides, Doominator had it coming. They *all* did."

"I guess you're right," his sister replied.

After Pep got over the shock of what had just happened, a smile slowly crept to her face as she realized how her life had suddenly changed. Doominator was dead, or irreparably damaged, anyway. Mrs. Higgins and the bowler dudes were still out there somewhere, but they didn't seem like such a threat anymore. And Dr. Warsaw was in police custody. The twins' long nightmare had come to an end.

And so had Skyride. At the bottom, Coke and Pep's parents were waiting for them. During the ride, they hadn't turned around to see what was going on in the chair behind them, so they had no idea that their children very nearly just died.

"Wasn't that fun?" asked Mrs. McDonald.

Coke and Pep looked at each other.

"Yeah!" they said simultaneously.

With Dr. Warsaw and his clone out of the way, the twins could cut loose. Joyland lived up to its name. Coke and Pep went on every ride in the park, even the kiddie rides. They had a fantastic time. Their parents had not seen such big smiles on their faces in a long, long time.

Finally, an announcement came over a loudspeaker

saying the park would close in thirty minutes.

"Let's blow this pop stand," Coke said.

As they got back on the road, everyone agreed that Texas was *amazing*. They had seen and done so many cool things. Mrs. McDonald, of course, made it a point to mention all the cool places they *hadn't* visited yet: Cadillac Ranch in Amarillo. The statue of a pig on wheels in Abilene. The Texas Surf Museum in Corpus Christi. The National Museum of Funeral History in Houston. The World's Largest Strawberry in Poteet. And they never made it to Hidalgo, the Killer Bee Capital of the World.

The McDonalds could have spent the entire summer in Texas. But it felt like the time was right to move on.

Heading west on Route 114 out of Lubbock, they soon passed through the appropriately named town of Levelland. Less than an hour later, this sign appeared at the side of the road:

"Woo-hoo!" Coke hollered. "Hey, did you guys know that New Mexico has more cattle than human beings?"

"Nobody cares, doofus," Pep said.

"The cows care," Coke replied. "Too bad they can't vote. They would take over."

Mrs. McDonald ceremoniously dropped her Texas guidebook into the trash bag and cracked open her brand-new copy of *New Mexico Off the Beaten Path.*

New Mexico is an amazing state with deep caves, red mountains, and thousand-year-old Indian villages. But right here it looked a lot like West Texas. Hot. Flat. Dry. Barren. As the McDonalds drove west on Route 380, there were no towns for seventy miles. Just nothingness. There was something peaceful about it.

Mrs. McDonald was a little worried. It was getting late, and they would need a place to stay for the night. It didn't look like there would be many motels out in the wilderness.

Shortly after they saw a sign for the Bitter Lake National Wildlife Refuge, evidence of civilization started to appear. Soon they were rolling into Roswell, otherwise known as the Dairy Capital of the World.

It was obvious. The town smelled like cows.

But you, reader, are probably aware that Roswell, New Mexico, is much more famous for something else—UFOs.

In the summer of 1947, the story goes, something fell out of the sky near Roswell. The Army said it was an experimental high-altitude balloon. But a lot of people insisted it was an extraterrestrial spacecraft. Not only that, but they said that some alien pilots were found inside the UFO, and the U.S. government performed medical experiments on them.

Whether or not aliens visited Roswell in 1947, the town hasn't been reluctant to take advantage of the controversy. As the McDonald family drove downtown through North Main Street, they passed three blocks crammed with alien-themed gift shops and attractions. Tourists were walking around wearing T-shirts with WE PROBE IN PEACE printed on them. The local Arby's has a sign that says ALIENS WELCOME. Streetlights are in the shape of alien heads. Even the McDonald's is shaped like a flying saucer.

"This place is cheesetastic!" Coke proclaimed.

"Cheesetastic?" asked Mrs. McDonald.

"Fantastically cheesy," Coke translated.

The International UFO Museum and Research Center had already closed for the day. Too bad. They have a model UFO, a film of the "official" autopsy of the alien bodies after the 1947 crash, and a prop alien-corpse dummy.

The Alien Zone was closed too. For a few dollars, you can go inside and take pictures of yourself next

265

to alien mannequins sitting at a bar, in a jail, in an outhouse, and at an alien autopsy scene.

"What a load of baloney," Dr. McDonald said as he drove past a street sign that said UFO PARKING ONLY.

"Oh, I don't know, honey," Mrs. McDonald said. "There are literally billions of planets in the universe. Who's to say for sure that ours is the only one that has intelligent life on it?"

"I am," Dr. McDonald said firmly.

"Lots of people say they've seen UFOs, Dad," Pep said. "Some of them even claim to have been abducted by aliens."

"Lunatics and nut jobs," her father replied. "Those crackpots are always drunk, by themselves, and out in the middle of nowhere when they spot UFOs. If aliens are so intelligent, they'd come to New York City or Los Angeles. Why don't they land on the White House lawn and introduce themselves?"

"Because we'd hit them with nuclear bombs and blow them to smithereens," Coke replied.

"I'll believe in UFOs when I see one with my own eyes," Dr. McDonald said.

Mrs. McDonald did a search for motels in Roswell, and there were plenty to choose from. She booked a room at the Best Western El Rancho Palacio, which was right up the street from Alien Zone.

"Check it out!" Coke said when the family walked around the back to their room. "They have a Ping-Pong table!"

It was an old wooden table that was out on the grass and unprotected against the elements. The edges had been chipped by frustrated players, but the table looked usable. Their parents said it was okay for the kids to play Ping-Pong while they themselves settled into their room. Coke grabbed paddles and Pep found a few balls in a trunk filled with board games and playing cards.

"Okay, volley for serve," Coke said.

Neither of the twins was great at Ping-Pong, but both were decent, and they were evenly matched. Soon the little ball was zipping back and forth across the table. The score was 8–7 when Coke slammed a shot that she couldn't reach to his sister's backhand

side. As Pep went to chase down the ball, she heard something—a strange humming sound in the distance. She stopped to listen.

"Did you hear that?" she asked.

"Hear *what*?"

"That sound," Pep said. "It was humming or vibrating or something."

"Probably an air conditioner," Coke said. "My serve."

"It came from over there," Pep said, pointing to the trees behind the motel. "Come on, follow me."

It was that strange time of day when it was starting to get dark on the ground but clouds could still be seen hanging in the sun's fading light. Still holding her paddle, Pep wandered toward the trees where she had heard the humming noise.

All was quiet except for a rustling in the trees. And then, suddenly, there was a louder vibration. Coke and Pep turned their heads to the left just in time to see this:

And then it was out of sight.

"Did you see *that*?" Coke asked. "What *was* it?"

"You think it was a—"

Pep never finished the sentence. Two powerful bluish beams of something—light? photons? energy?—came down from the sky directly overhead like spotlights, illuminating and enveloping the twins. When Coke and Pep tried to step away from the beams, something prevented them from moving their legs. They closed their eyes to shield them from the blinding light, but they could still see it through their eyelids. Pep reached out instinctively to take her brother's hand.

That's when their feet lifted up off the ground.

EPILOGUE

Wait! What? Did Coke and Pep just get abducted by aliens? I sure didn't see *that* coming. What happens now? Are they going to get sucked up into the alien spacecraft? What happens when their parents find they are missing? Will the twins be taken to the aliens' planet? What will the aliens do to them? Will Coke and Pep ever return to Earth? The answer is . . .

You'll just have to wait for *The Genius Files #5* to find out.

I'll tell you one thing, though. It's going to be a wild ride.

ABOUT THE AUTHOR

Besides The Genius Files, Dan Gutman is the author of the My Weird School series, the Baseball Card Adventure series, and many other books for young readers. Dan lives in New Jersey. To find out more about him and his books, go to www.dangutman.com.

Join the McDonald twins on their death-defying
cross-country adventure in

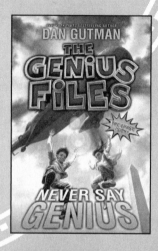